ISBN-13: 978-1-952412-17-2

Cover design: https://100covers.com/
Published By: Vagabond Publishing
Printed in the United States of America

1

The small café was only half full at nine a.m., the mid-December weather too frosty for the large crowds of tourists that flocked to La Villita every year near downtown San Antonio. That made it a perfect time for me to stop in for one of the best breakfasts in town, only a few blocks away from my small office. The pancakes were fluffy, the eggs were scrambled just right, and the bacon was soft with crispy edges.

I ate at the café most mornings and craved the meal on the days I couldn't stop in because of pressing business elsewhere. While sitting at a small table, my eyes were often drawn to the historic small plaza outside the window in between pages of whatever book I was currently reading on my phone. For that one hour I was at total peace with the world, completely relaxed.

Which made it all the more annoying when a shadow fell across my table as someone stood between me and the view outside the window. I kept my head down, eyes scanning an electronic page, hoping it was just the waitress coming to check on me. After the shadow hadn't moved and the person hadn't spoken for half a minute, I sighed internally and looked up.

The woman standing only a few feet away was in her mid to late forties, thin to the point of emaciation even with a light jacket covering her arms and chest. Her long brown hair showed gray roots, framing brown eyes that focused on mine the instant I looked up, refusing to let go with their intense gaze.

"Can I help you?" I asked, trying to put as much *I don't want to be bothered* into my tone as possible.

The woman either didn't notice or pretended not to. She only took a hesitant step forward and bent down to speak quietly with her heavy accent. "Are you him? The man that can solve unusual problems?"

And just like that, my calm breakfast hour was cut drastically short. I pushed aside my half eaten plate, and waved the woman to the chair across from me. "I'm Jack Dahlish. Why don't you tell me your name and what made you seek me out?"

She sat almost daintily on the chair across the table from me, placing just her fingertips on the edge of the table as she leaned forward. "I'm Amalia Fuentes. My granddaughter is missing, Mr. Dahlish, and the police have been unable to help us. One of the policemen told me I should find you. He said *you* could help us."

"When did the girl go missing? Which police officer mentioned me?" There were a lot of questions already fighting in my head after the short statements, but I started with the two I felt were most important.

"My daughter, Anna, she took little Penny to the park in the morning to play on the slides. It's her favorite place in the world. She can go up the little stairs to slide down over and over again for as long as you will let her." The woman smiled sadly at the memory. "Anna was talking with one of the other mothers, letting Penny play with the other children while looking after her now and then. When half an hour had passed and it was time to leave, Anna called out for my grandbaby. But she was nowhere to be found. The other mothers helped her look, but there was no sign of Penny. No one could remember seeing her leave the play-ground at all."

Amalia reached over to pull a napkin from a small stack on the table, holding it to each eye to dry the tears that had started to slide down her cheeks as she told the story. "They called the police right away, and two officers searched the park and sur-rounding neighborhood but couldn't find Penny. More police ar-rived and helped with the search, but that was three days ago. They've found nothing, Mr. Dahlish. No one has come forward saying they saw her leave the park or at any time after, and we have heard nothing at all!" The tears were flowing more heavily now, and a few diners two tables over kept looking askance at the woman.

"Yesterday, I went to the police station and demanded an-swers. My little Penny has been missing for three days, Mr. Dahlish, and all they can say is that they have no leads. Anna does not like that I am so pushy with the police, but I know that if I don't keep after them then they will forget about us. Just another little Mexican baby lost, and no one will care but the family who is left without answers." The woman was getting angry now, her eyes accusing as they looked at me. She saw just another Cauca-sian man in front of her, one slightly taller than average with short dark hair and pale blue eyes, representative of all those who wouldn't care about her grief because of her heritage.

She calmed after a few moments, though, remembering that she had come to me for help. "A nice officer, a man who said I should call him Ollie, told me that he believed the police could not help us. He said that I should see you, because my Penny going missing is something you would be able to help me with."

Ollie Williams was an officer I knew pretty well, a sergeant I met almost a decade before when I was in much the same situation as Amalia Fuentes and her family. Before I knew what kind of dangers lay hidden in the world around us. Ollie had been old for a street cop even then, his tight black hair more than half gray over a chocolate brown face that housed a multitude of wrinkles that told the story of many days spent smiling and laughing with his unending good humor. All these years later, he was still working the streets of San Antonio, refusing any promotion above sergeant and determined to serve the people directly instead of trying to do it from behind a desk. He and I had worked together on quite a few cases since I met him, and he was one of the few people who knew the truth about the kinds of issues I dealt with in my work.

"If Ollie sent you my way, then I'm probably the one to help you." I looked more carefully at the woman, wondering how deep I should go down the rabbit hole with her. I decided to keep it general for now, and take a look at the issue to see what I could find. Amalia wrote down her phone number on a piece of paper in the small notebook I carried everywhere, and also gave me her daughter's name and telephone number. I promised I would spend the day looking into the disappearance.

Amalia looked at me with a frown for several seconds after I finished speaking, her lips twisting. "I do not have much money to pay you," she said finally, almost apologetically. "My Anna has nothing, she barely gets by since she is raising a child on her own."

"Mrs. Fuentes, I'm not asking for any money," I told her, trying to put as much reassurance as possible in my voice. "Let me take a look around the park and talk to Anna, and I'll call you

4

tonight to let you know if I think I can help you. We can talk about payment then, but I promise I will never ask for more than you can give."

Rising from the table, I dropped enough cash to pay for my meal and leave a nice tip for the waitress watching from near the kitchen behind a veil of long black hair. Amalia rose with me, still wiping at her eyes with the napkin and looking around in embarrassment as she realized several people were watching us. I walked with her out of the café, and we stood in the morning sun on the lightly trafficked pedestrian walkway.

"You will call tonight?" she asked, as if reassuring herself.

"I promise I'll call, Mrs. Fuentes," I told her. "Even if this isn't the sort of problem I usually handle, that alone will be good information for Ollie to know so the cops can refocus their investigation."

"Why did Sergeant Williams think you can help me if the police can't, Mr. Dahlish? What is your sort of problem?"

Chuckling, I slid my phone into a back pocket of my jeans and started to turn away. "We'll discuss that if we need to, tomorrow. I'll talk to you later, Mrs. Fuentes." I shoved my hands into my pockets, putting my head down to walk against the chill morning wind that had blown up while I was in the café. I had left my jacket at home, lulled by the forecast of sun and warmth that would be coming in the afternoon, but the walk back to my office was no more than a couple of blocks. As I walked, I thought about the missing little girl and wondered why Ollie had sent the grandmother to see me. He must have thought it important if he told her where to look for me in case I wasn't in my office. Calling him moved up in my mental list.

Entering the small lobby of the historic Tower Life building always felt like stepping back in time. The building had been constructed in the late 1920s, and the neo-gothic styling of the exterior and lobby were reminiscent of what I had always felt to be the grand golden days of American architecture. Modern glass towers had a beauty of their own, but the time and skill that went into the stonework of the buildings in the late nineteenth and early twentieth century granted an elegance and style that would never fade. The lobby had high vaulted ceilings and arched doorways that were very reminiscent of old European churches. Marble tile covered the floor, leading into a bank of elevators with shining brass doors that looked almost as I imagined they must have when the building opened in 1929.

My own small office was halfway up the tower, giving me a view of several open-air parking areas and a smaller more modern office building that blocked my view of the charming La Villita. Which is partly how I'd gotten a decent rate on the lease. I had enough space for two rooms, the first a small sitting area that I'd spent hours furnishing and decorating when I had dreams of clients waiting to speak with me.

The office beyond that was simply appointed. A small wooden desk in the middle of the room, holding my laptop, coffee cup, and an old picture of my sister. Two file cabinets sat to one side and a small storage closet opposite where I kept sensitive items locked away behind a heavy door. There were two armless chairs on the client side of my desk, growing a bit dusty from lack of use. The swivel chair I dropped into was the most expensive item in the small suite, a specially designed chair that I had ordered from the internet and spent far too much money on. However, it was the most comfortable chair I had ever owned.

While the laptop was booting, I pulled out my phone and scrolled through my contacts list to find Ollie's number. I hit the button to dial him as I typed in my extremely complex password to access the laptop. It was four letters and two numbers, exactly the kind of thing everyone tells you not to do. But it had worked marvelously through a decade of different computers. I certainly wouldn't be forgetting it and scrambling to find the piece of paper I'd scrawled it on in the early days after moving into the office.

"SAPD, Officer Williams speaking."

"Ollie," I said happily. "Did you catch the Spurs last night?"

"Hey, Jack. That was a great game. Looks like we might even make the playoffs again this year." Ollie paused, and I could almost feel his smile through the phone. "Did Mrs. Fuentes track you down?"

"Yes, and thank you so much for telling her how to find me. At least I'd made it halfway through my pancakes before she showed up."

"You know I wouldn't do something like that unless it was important, Jack." I could hear Ollie's voice getting rougher as the smile left his tone. In his mid-fifties, with grandchildren of his own, the veteran officer knew very well the kind of grief that could be felt when a child was missing.

"I know, Ollie. Amalia told me about her granddaughter going missing. Three days is a long time for a child to be gone. Have there been any leads at all?"

"Not a damn thing. It's like the little girl just turned around and disappeared in the blink of an eye. I knocked on a few dozen doors myself that first day, and no one saw any sign of her. There hasn't even been the usual crank calls on the tip lines."

I grunted at that, knowing just how many false leads and crazy confessions the police had to comb through with every crime that was reported in the press. A quick web search found several stories on local news sites detailing the search for Penelope Castillo. I also saw my first picture of the young girl, her brown hair up in pigtails as she smiled widely at the camera with the tip of her tongue sticking out between her teeth. I could imagine her giggles at whoever was behind the camera, and couldn't help but feel a deep well of sympathy for the girl's mother and grandmother.

"So, what made you send her my way? What is it about this disappearance that makes you think it's my kind of problem?"

Ollie was quiet for several moments, and I thought he must be striding down a hallway to find an out of the way place to talk where he wouldn't be overheard. When he did speak, his voice was pitched low. "Go to the park, Jack. It's Dawson Park, out near the arena. I felt something there when we were taking the report after the kid went missing, and it gave me the shivers. Honestly, it reminded me a lot of what I felt that day we first met."

It was my turn to be silent, and I could feel my jaw clenching as I remembered that day beside the small pond. A day that had been the worst moment of my life, and also my last day of living like a normal person. "That bad, huh? I'm heading over there shortly, before I visit the mother. She lives close by, right?"

"Only two blocks up, a nice house for that neighborhood. I'd swing by and walk it with you, but they have me working with some rookie to follow up on reports of suspicious activity at a jewelry store up north."

"No reason to pull you away just to stand in a park with me," I told him. "I'll call you later today, let you know if I find anything."

After hanging up, I considered whether to call Anna and ask if she would see me. I decided to hold off until later. In my experience, you can see more truth when you surprise someone the first time you meet. I set the phone down and returned to my search of the news posts and videos about the little girl's disappearance. Several locals were interviewed, adamant that no one in their neighborhood could be responsible for something like a child abduction. I didn't even want to run a search of pedophiles in the area to see how wrong they were. Something like that would never have driven Ollie to recommend me to Amalia.

A link at the bottom of one page grabbed my attention. It was a story listed under Related Items, two months old and detailing another child abduction on the west side of the city. Out of curiosity, I clicked the link and watched the short clip. A reporter with bright red lipstick that almost matched her fiery hair walked slowly through a deserted park, hands held in front of her as she spoke.

"The four-year-old was playing here, on the swing set, enjoying a warm October afternoon in the park. For her mother, that sunny day was the start of a nightmare."

Such clichéd crap, I couldn't help thinking. No one had ever been able to explain to me why every reporter seemed to find it necessary to speak in high drama all the time. This story was one that warranted it, I had to admit. Another small girl, playing in a busy park, who disappeared without a trace. It was the kind of story that made me start to wonder how often children go missing and are forgotten by everyone but their families after a twenty-four-hour news cycle.

After reading through a few more stories about Penny's disappearance, I decided it was time to go see the park. I patted my pocket to make sure my car keys were still there, grabbed my phone, and hoped that traffic would have cleared out for the short drive.

2

Traffic had not cleared out. Thanks in large part to road construction that had Commerce Street narrowed down to one lane. Several drivers at a standstill in front of me were yelling at the road workers, blaming them for being late to work or appointments. I took the opportunity to turn up the classic rock station and lean back against the cool faux leather headrest. The sun was shining down, warming the interior of my car even as the weather outside continued to grow colder. For the hundredth time that morning, I cursed myself for not pulling up a more recent weather report before leaving my small home.

Half an hour later I parked in the deserted lot beside the park, and climbed out of my well-worn Honda. Only two other spaces were taken, a minivan and small hatchback that looked to belong to the large family kicking a ball around on the brown winter grass. A breeze blew in, causing me to wrap my arms tightly around my chest. It seemed as if the city's respite from winter was coming to an end for at least a few days.

The playground was close to the parking lot, and I crossed to stand on the edge of it. A yellow canopy high above shielded playing children from the hot Texas summer sun or occasional rain showers. The ground was covered with shredded brown mulch material, which seemed to be mostly rubber when I stepped down onto it. My feet bounced a bit on the material, no doubt meant to protect small bodies from the inevitable falls.

There were a variety of places for kids to play, all connected by short bridges with high yellow railings. Ladders of several types to climb, a couple of curving slides, a pole with a corkscrew design that made it easy for small legs to climb, a rubber swinging bridge to cross between two solid platforms. It kind of made me envious to look at all the possibilities represented in the small playground. When I was small, we had a couple of swings and a seesaw. And we were happy to have that much.

"Oh, God," I muttered. "I'm turning into dad."

Amalia had mentioned that Penny loved the slides, so I circled around to approach them. Within a few feet I could feel a cold sensation crawling up from my legs, and goosebumps broke out across my skin. Reaching up to touch the talisman I wore under my shirt at all times, I closed my eyes.

Opening myself slightly to the sensation, it felt as if the air were swirling around me. Even on a day growing progressively cooler, this area of the playground was infinitely colder to someone able to recognize the darkness and shadows left behind by an evil presence. There was a musky taste on the air, one that snuck into the back of my throat and almost made me gag.

The girl had been missing for three days, and I had no reason to think that whatever had taken her would return to the playground. To be able to feel its presence so strongly after that length of time, I knew I was dealing with a powerful being. Any hope of a pervy pedophile lurking around and snatching Penny at an opportune moment was blown away. Opening my eyes, I experienced a few moments of being trapped within a cyclone of dark smoke before it blew away and the sunlight rushed in.

Whatever had left this trace behind, it was something I had never dealt with before.

Whatever doubts I'd harbored about this case not being one of mine were gone. I felt a desire to push forward and find the solution to this problem. After a decade of tracking and stopping almost every kind of threat unimaginable to the vast majority of humanity, it had grown increasingly rare for me to find something new. To discover it less than three miles from the office I worked out of almost every day, less than five miles from the old home I had purchased years before... that was almost terrifying.

Two blocks north of the park, I strolled along the sidewalk looking at the houses on either side of me. This part of the neighborhood had a calm and peaceful feeling about it, the sort of aura that made young couples want to move in and raise their children there. A cloud of pain and anger was almost palpable around one house as I approached it, strong enough that I could never understand how no one else could experience such things.

I took a deep breath as I turned to walk up the carefully tended path to the bright yellow front door. The facade of the house was rust colored red brick below, with old but recently repainted yellow siding above. Along with green trim around the roof, the colors gave the house an almost festive look. Carefully trimmed plants and bushes were planted to either side of the small porch. I couldn't help but wonder what kind of colors they'd display in the spring when flowers were blooming.

My hand was raised to press the bell when the door swung open violently. A large Hispanic man was standing behind the barred screen door, several inches taller and at least fifty pounds heavier than I was. His shaved head and braided goatee made him even more intimidating.

"We already told you vultures that we ain't giving interviews," he said, raising a hand to shoo me away. "Get off the porch, vato, and don't come back."

I didn't budge, except to pull a crisp business card from a back pocket. They may be going the way of the dodo and the dinosaurs, but I found they could open doors that would otherwise stay closed. Literally, in this case, as the man cracked the screen door open just enough to grab the card and crumple it up in his large fist.

"My name is Jack Dahlish. Amalia Fuentes has asked me to look into the disappearance of her granddaughter. I was hoping I could speak with Anna for a few minutes."

With raised eyebrows, the man smoothed out the business card and looked it over carefully. "What are you, some kind of private detective?"

"Sort of," I said with a hopeful smile.

A moment later the screen door was pushed open and the man stepped aside to let me enter the tidy home. The living room just inside the door was filled with soft couches and chairs, with pictures covering the walls. A young woman that featured in most of them looked like a younger version of Amalia, with the small girl that I recognized as Penny from the news stories often sharing the frame.

"I'm Emilio," the man said, breezing past to sit in a worn leather recliner. "Sorry for the rough greeting, but we've had reporters at the door constantly the last few days."

"Anna's brother?" I asked, hazarding a guess.

He laughed, shaking his head. "Sort of," he replied, turning my vague answer against me. "Penny's dad is my brother."

Sitting on a couch near him, I leaned forward in interest. "Is the girl's father still around? Amalia didn't mention him at all."

"Nah, she wouldn't. Amalia and Michael don't get along so well these days." Emilio pursed his lips for a moment, and then shrugged. "But Michael hasn't been around for a few years. He's up in Huntsville."

I was shocked to hear that. The town was known for only one thing. "Death row?"

Laughing and slapping at the arm of the recliner, he shook his head until he could catch his breath to answer. "Nah, homie. Different unit up there. He got fourteen years for armed robbery of a bank. Stupid pendejo."

"Emilio! Watch your language." A woman entered from a dark hallway, stopping when she saw me. The woman from the photos. I rose to greet her, holding out a hand as I introduced myself. "I'm sorry, Mr. Dahlish. My mother didn't mention she had talked with you."

"No, ma'am. I asked her not to, until I had a chance to meet you myself."

Anna eyed me carefully as she sat on the edge of a chair that was on the other side of a scratched coffee table. "Do you think you can find my Penny?"

"I'm certainly going to try, Mrs. Castillo."

"Fuentes," she said quickly. "Michael and I aren't married, but we used his name for our daughter."

"Ms. Fuentes," I corrected. "To start out, I'd like to hear about the day Penny went missing. I want your perspective on what happened."

She looked at me for half a minute before coming to a decision, launching into her story. "It was Saturday morning. Penny was sitting there watching her cartoons while I was cleaning up in the kitchen." She pointed at the cushion beside me, the best vantage point for the small television that faced the seating area. "When her favorite cartoons were over, she begged me to take her to the park. She'd made some friends there a while back, and she was always wanting to go see if they were around to play with. I made her wait until I finished cleaning, and it was around 9:30 when we left to walk down to Dawson." Anna was looking at an empty hook between two light winter coats that must have belonged to her and Emilio.

"When we got to the park, there were six or seven other kids playing. Penny ran off to join them, always trying to fit in with the older kids." She paused to smile sadly, producing a tissue that had been tucked into a long sleeve, using it to wipe her eyes. "I sat on a bench and watched her play. Another mother was there, a woman I've seen a few times from the next street over. We started to talk about the weather, our plans for the weekend, things like that. I was enjoying myself too much, getting to be around another adult. I took my eyes off my baby, and she never came back."

As the woman broke down in tears, Emilio rose from the recliner to stand beside her chair and run a hand over her back. I could hear him whispering comforting words to her, a promise that he would be there for her. Rising to cross the room, I stood in front of a wall of pictures. There was Penny as a newborn, swaddled in her mother's arms with a heavyset man covered in tattoos beside her. Penny blowing out a single candle on a pink birthday cake, mother and father looking down on her with joy. Penny riding one of the horses on springs that I had seen earlier in the park, only her mother at her side with a troubled smile.

"I'm sorry, Mr. Dahlish. I feel so silly when I cry like that."

"Jack, please." Taking a seat on the couch again, I leaned forward with my elbows on my knees. "Never be ashamed for feeling as much love as you do for your daughter. A parent's love is the greatest gift any child can have."

She nodded gratefully, blowing her nose in the tissue before tucking it away again.

"Anna, where was the last place you saw Penny? Can you remember?"

"Well, I looked up once and saw her going down the slide. That was on the opposite side of the playset from the bench, so it's hard to see much over there once they slide down from the top." She closed her eyes and furrowed her brows, trying to relive the morning. "We were talking about pies, then. The other mother belongs to our church, and there's a bake sale this weekend. So we were discussing which pies we planned to bake for that."

Anna's eyes shot open and her arm reached out, as if to grab something in front of her. "I heard Penny yell! How could I have forgotten that? It was a short little scream, the kind she would give when Emilio tossed her in the air or pushed her really fast down the street on her bike."

"And you didn't see her again after that?"

17

"No. I'm sure I didn't. Mr. Dahlish, was that when she was taken? Was my baby in trouble and I didn't even know it?"

"We can't know that for sure, Anna. She could have just been enjoying a really fun trip down the slide." The lies rolled off my tongue, and I could only hope she believed them easier than I could. Somehow, I knew that the girl's scream was her very last moment of freedom. I just had to hope that I could find whatever took her at that moment, and return her safely to this pleasant little home that any kid would love to grow up in.

I glanced at Emilio before my last question, making sure he knew I was including them both. "Can you think of anyone who might want to hurt you by taking Penny? Any estranged family members, or friends that you've had a falling out with?"

"Yo, man. The cops already asked us about this stuff." Emilio was getting angry as he spoke, which I thought was an interesting reaction.

"Tell me what you told the cops. Then think about it for a few seconds, and give me the answer you would never tell the police."

Emilio stood up from the recliner again, stomping to the other side of the small room. "Ain't nobody that would want to hurt Penny. And anyone who doesn't like me would never make the mistake of trying to pick on my family."

Anna didn't even react to the outburst, her eyes remaining on mine. "When Michael was caught after the bank robbery, the cops were always asking me who his friends were. No one said it, but I think they felt one of the people with him got away. I don't know why that person might want to hurt my baby, but it's the only thing I could think of when the detectives asked us this on Saturday."

It would be a good lead to follow, or at least to ask Ollie about. I felt sure the police were already looking into anything like that. "Emilio? Just give me a name. There's always at least one person."

He rounded on me, jabbing a finger in the air. "Oh yeah? You got people in your life that don't like you and would want to hurt you by taking a little kid?"

"It would take a few days for me to list out everyone in that category. I've made a lot of enemies in my life, more than most people. That's how I know there's always someone on everyone's list."

Emilio's mouth moved with disgust, and he almost spat the words out. "Tyson Blake. I was in a gang when I was young and stupid, back in high school. Tyson was a kid in my class who belonged to a rival gang. Cabrón always had it in for me, even jumped me a few times after school. But I haven't seen that asshole in two years, man."

"It's a place to start, at least. Which gang were you in?"

"La Calavera. It was a nothing little gang, only five or six teenagers thinking we were hot shit."

Thanking them both for speaking with me, I rose and placed a fresh card on the coffee table. "I'll call you tomorrow, and let you know if I've found anything. In the meantime, if you think of anything that might be important or remember something from what we discussed today, call me. The ringer is always off so it doesn't interrupt moments like this, but leave me a message and I'll call you right back.

"I can't promise that I'll find Penny, but I do promise that I'm going to work as hard as I possibly can and do everything in my power to that end."

Walking back to the park to retrieve my car, I felt sure that Anna was not involved in her child's disappearance. Most people would get angry at me for even suggesting such a thing, but I knew all too well how often parents were driven to do despicable things by desperation or addiction.

Emilio had given off a good aura, as well, though there were some dark waves around him that I'd have to look into. Perhaps it was just his flirtation with gang life as a kid, or just an echo of his brother's deeds.

Michael Castillo would bear some investigation. Ollie could fill me in on anything the police had on his past before the bank robbery, and should also be able to give me a rundown on this missing accomplice. That would seem to be a very mundane situation, but finding the supernatural in the last place you expected was not all that uncommon.

3

"**M**onsters are real."

Amalia Fuentes sat in a recently dusted chair across the desk. I called her early in the afternoon to tell her I was willing to look into Penny's disappearance. She'd been so happy that she rushed over to meet me at my office. The office was dimly lit with the late afternoon sun on the far side of the building, so much so that I had turned on a few small lamps. Amalia sat with her legs crossed at the ankle and tucked under the chair, her bony hands clasped whitely in her lap. My words had caused her to look at me with perplexed confusion.

"They are real, and one of them took your granddaughter. I'm going to do everything I can to bring her back to you, but I can't make any promises."

Her brows were furrowed, and I could see that she wanted to ask many questions. She settled on the one most important to her. "Who do you think did it, Mr. Dahlish?"

"Jack, please." I ran a hand over the smooth surface of my desk. "After talking with your daughter and Emilio, I have several places to start looking."

Amalia's lips tightened, and she turned her shoulders away from me. "You should start with that Emilio. He is hanging around Anna and Penny far too much to be decent. That whole family is bad."

"You don't like Michael?"

"I did, at first. He and Anna met in high school, when she was a sophomore and he was a senior. Michael seemed like such a nice boy back then, soft spoken and courteous. He would always have my Anna back home before the curfew, and he never acted inappropriately that I could see." She crossed her arms, hugging them close to her chest as she spoke.

"When my husband died, four years ago, Michael was there for me and Anna. She had just graduated from high school, and I thank God that Benito got to see that before he passed. I fell apart for a while, Mr. Dahlish. But Michael would stop by every evening to cook us a meal and help around the house. He was working as a mechanic, putting in long hours there before spending the evening with me and Anna.

"The day she told me she was pregnant, I hugged them both so hard. I thought for sure they would get married, move in together, and start a family. But Michael, he said he was not made for such things. He moved Anna into his home, but would not make her his wife." Amalia's nose wrinkled as she spat out the last words. "I believe that even then he was doing illegal things, stealing from people. And it makes me sick to think that some of that money was spent on me because I was in such a bad way after Benito died."

"Were there any signs that he was committing crimes, before he got arrested for the bank robbery?"

"None at all, or at least none that I could see. Anna swears he was talked into going along that time by his friends. You know the people caught with him were all from his work?"

"Everyone he worked with was involved?"

She shrugged, and I could tell it wasn't something she'd spent much time considering. "I don't know. Three of them were caught with him after robbing the bank, though. Anna and I sat through the trial for two weeks, little Penny not even a year old. I will never be able to forgive Michael for what he did to my daughter and granddaughter. Not ever."

I decided to hold off on more questions about the robbery until I had a chance to speak with Ollie. His phone had gone straight to voicemail earlier, and I had texted to ask him to meet me later that night. I was hoping to see him in a few hours and get more of the story behind the bank robbery.

"Amalia, is there anyone you can think of that would want to hurt you or Anna? Or maybe someone that would take Penny to try and hurt you?"

"No! Why would anyone want to take a little girl to hurt me?"

"I have to ask. You would be surprised how often child abductions are done by someone close to the family."

"There is no one in our family who would do this. It is just me and Anna now."

"No siblings? Aunts or uncles around the area? Cousins?"

She laughed bitterly. "Just because I am Hispanic, it does not mean that I have a large family."

"I didn't mean to imply anything like that," I said.

"People always think it. I was an only child, and my parents died many years ago. Benito had a brother, but I never met him. Lives up in Colorado or Wyoming, if I remember correctly. They didn't get along as kids, and I think they only talked once or twice after going their separate ways."

"Okay, thank you for putting up with my questions. I know you've probably answered them for the cops already, but it helps to get the information from you. I'm going to call Anna tomorrow, and give her an update on anything I'm able to find. You will be my very next call, I promise."

"Thank you, Mr. Dahlish. I hope you are able to find Penny, but even if you can't it feels good to know that someone is really looking." She grabbed her purse and dug around for a few moments. The checkbook she pulled out was scratched and worn, the cover jostled by years of purse contents. "How much will you charge me?"

This was the part of the job I always hated the most. Asking for money made me feel dirty, but I knew I couldn't keep helping people without the funds to do so. "I'll need a five hundred dollar retainer. My rate for this case is fifteen dollars per hour, with expenses. When I find Penny, or when you tell me to stop looking, we'll discuss how much more I need beyond the retainer."

Amalia was silent as she wrote out a check. Her writing was beautiful and flowed smoothly across the paper. It made me envious when I thought about my chicken scratch that even I had trouble reading sometimes. Once she finished writing, the check was carefully torn from the book and passed across my desk.

We stood together, and I walked around the desk to escort her out to the hallway. "You'll hear from me no later than five tomorrow afternoon. If you have anything you want to ask or discuss before then, feel free to call me. I'm working for you now, so I'm here for whatever you need."

"Thank you, Mr. Dahlish." Amalia smoothed her blouse as she walked through the door I held open, and I watched until she was at the end of the hall and entering the elevator.

Stepping across the office quickly, I gathered up my phone and shut down my computer before leaving. My next stop was half a mile away, and it was going to be a cold walk. Luckily, I had remembered to stop in at my house after visiting the park. I slid my arms into the long gray herringbone coat, buttoning it tightly and lifting the collar. The temperature had dropped nearly twenty degrees during the day, and it was forty-five degrees in the late afternoon sunlight.

Leaving the old building, I headed north for a couple of blocks before quickly running down a curving flight of stairs. Beside the river and out of the chill wind, it felt a little warmer. As I walked along behind crowds of tourists, I was able to let my mind wander over everything I'd learned during the day. The dark and cold feeling in the park made me confident that something supernatural was behind the disappearance. I just couldn't see it as a random act, and felt sure that there was a motive behind it. It might take a lot of digging to find the answer, but I was more than willing to do it.

Arriving at my destination, I walked down five stone steps worn by thousands of feet. The small establishment was almost hidden among the bright and glittering restaurants and bars that lined the Riverwalk. Unlike them, Lyon's Den was not a place that wanted tourists wandering in. A few inevitably did every weekend but most left after a quick drink at the gleaming ash bar, sensing that they weren't welcome.

When I entered the long low-ceilinged room, there were several people hunched over drinks at the bar. The half dozen small tables along the opposite wall were empty, as they usually were unless it was very busy. No one looked around as the heavy door thumped behind me. It was warm inside, so I pulled off my coat and tossed it over a stool. Climbing onto the one next to it, I smacked my palm on the varnished bar top a few times.

"Yeah, yeah. I heard you come in, Jack." The man who approached behind the bar was a few inches over my six foot height, with long reddish brown hair swept back from his forehead. His shoulders were broad and straight, his body thin but strong.

"Hey, Richard. I'll have whatever is new this week." The bartender and owner of the Den was always buying a keg or two of different local brews each week. With microbreweries popping up all over central Texas, he never repeated the local special for more than two weeks at a time. A tall glass filled with a light amber ale was put down in front of me, an inch of foam at the top. "Seen Ollie today?"

"Haven't seen the cop in a few weeks, Jack. Expecting him?"

I nodded as I was taking a big swallow of the beer, my eyes darting across the other patrons at the bar. The man seven stools away hunched down even more as he felt my eyes. Terrance was a two-bit hustler, running scams on tourists along the Riverwalk most days. He was also a half-goblin, born to a human mother. Straddling both worlds made him an outcast most times. Humans felt uncomfortable around him for reasons they couldn't understand, and the creatures of the Filii Nox saw him as an abomination.

"Remember the rules, Jack," Richard said under his breath, wiping at the spotless bar with a clean rag. I grunted in acknowledgement. The Den had been established in 1949, a safe haven for humans and Nox alike. I raised my beer in Terrance's direction, a silent apology for my long stare.

Richard headed back to the far end of the bar, where a man and woman were talking with their heads close together. As the barman entered the conversation, my curiosity flared. The pair were unknown to me, and I tried to figure out if they were locals or visiting from out of town. They never even glanced in my direction, which was odd in itself since I was well known among the local Nox and few humans who knew about the supernatural creatures.

A hand dropped onto my shoulder, and I jumped. A bit of beer splashed on the shining bar, earning me a glare from Richard. I wiped up the spill with a napkin as rich laughter poured out beside me.

"A little jumpy today, Jack?" Ollie asked as he sat on an adjacent stool.

"Lost in thought," I said, as Richard approached to wipe up the spilled beer that had eluded my ineffectual napkin. "Another one for the sergeant, please, Richard."

"I could use it," Ollie said through a deep sigh. "People my age should not be saddled with eager beaver rookies."

"Too much energy for you to keep up with?"

"Yeah, and too many questions about every little thing. 'Why did you bag a candy wrapper, sergeant?' 'Why didn't you ask the witness more questions, sergeant?'" He took a deep gulp of the beer placed before him, wiping the foam from his upper lip.

"Then I got a ten minute lecture on how she was taught to do things differently in the academy. Apparently, old farts like me should have to go back and take classes to keep up with advances in technology and procedure."

"Didn't you just spend two weeks up in Austin last summer taking those kinds of courses?"

"Sure did. Even taught one of them to the robbery and homicide detectives in SAPD last fall."

I laughed, which quickly turned into a groan. "I hate that I'm already old enough to say this... but kids these days are such know-it-all assholes."

"Millennials," Ollie said through a wide smile. "Give them a few years, and they'll be complaining about the next generation instead of those that came before them."

"How long are you stuck with the rookie? Think she'll make it through the six-month probation period?"

His salt and pepper head nodded. "She's a good kid, just new to the job and still thinking that she already learned everything there is to know. It was supposed to be a temporary assignment, but it sounds like her training officer is going to be out on medical leave for a while. With no one else available, I think I'm stuck with her for the duration."

Grimacing, I took a sip from my half empty glass. Having a rookie around everywhere he went would limit my ability to work with Ollie when I ran into a difficult case. Or when I needed to call him for information.

"As much as I'm enjoying the beer, why did you want to see me, Jack?" It was like he was reading my mind, as his dark eyes turned to look at me.

"I went down to Dawson Park today. You were right about there being something non-human involved in the disappearance. I could feel an essence of something I've never encountered before very close to where Penny was taken."

"Was it the same thing as that day at the pond?" His question was quiet, almost hesitant to bring up the bad memories I still suffered from that first meeting and the subsequent events.

"No, this was something I've never felt before. I'm going to have to do some research and see if I can find any descriptions that match what I experienced today." Taking a sip, I pulled the small notebook from a rear pocket. "I talked to Anna and Emilio afterwards, and they brought up a few things I wanted to ask you about."

"Emilio? Shaved head, tall?"

"Yeah, that's him. You guys didn't talk to him during the investigation?"

Ollie sniffed in wry amusement. "That homie didn't say a word, just stood there glaring at us the entire time we were talking with Ms. Fuentes. What was his story?"

"He's the brother of the girl's father, Michael Castillo. They told me Michael was arrested for armed robbery almost three years ago, and that the police thought there might be another accomplice that got away?"

"Ah, Michael Castillo." Ollie's eyes were distant as he went over his memories of the case. "I wasn't involved in that one, but the gossip was all over the station when it happened. The FBI were even called in to lead the investigation because it was a national bank. If I remember correctly, Castillo was the man on the door, watching for any cops while three others committed the actual robbery. That's why he only got fourteen years while they all got the maximum sentence.

"The feds knew there was another person involved, but they could never get the others to flip on the driver of the getaway car. It was a bank branch up north of 410, with lots of shops and office buildings all around. Not the kind of place you plan to get away from on foot. They never recovered all the stolen money, either. About fifty grand is still missing."

"They didn't find anything to point them in the direction of that other accomplice? There had to be video cameras all over the place."

"Oh yeah, they found a great video. The morons parked their car twenty feet from an ATM, with the camera pointed right at the vehicle as they all got out and pulled on their masks. That video was the overwhelming evidence that the prosecution used to get such strong sentences. No view of the driver, though." Ollie shrugged, draining the last of his beer. Richard raised his head, silently asking if the sergeant wanted another drink. Ollie waved him off as he continued the story. "The make and model of the car were clear as day, as were the plates. When the feds tracked it down, though, they found that it had been in the shop for a brake job that day."

I groaned and put my head in my hands. "Let me guess. It was the same shop that Michael Castillo worked at?"

"Bingo. The three other robbers all worked there, as well. There were two more people who worked at the shop, so the feds focused on them pretty hard. I think we're still all convinced one or both had to be in on the robbery, but there was no way to prove it. They alibied each other, claiming to be at the shop working on a transmission rebuild together."

"No doubt they were ready to alibi the guys who robbed the bank, too."

"Three guys, one girl. Don't be a misogynist, Jack."

I glanced over to see the grin on his face. "Fine, alibi the guys *and girl* who robbed the bank."

"We'll never know for sure, but I'd bet heavily on it. The feds took along an SAPD robbery detective for the interview, and the genius blurted out that they had video of the robbers. Two questions in, before they could ask about alibis."

"That seems a little odd. Was he new to the job or something?"

"Nope, six years on the squad. The captain chewed him a new one, and the feds swore they would never work with the guy again. I don't know if he was on the take, or just got stupid while trying to impress the FBI."

There was silence for a few minutes as I thought about everything Ollie had told me. His cop eyes were scanning the other patrons in the bar, just as I had upon entering. Two more patrons had entered the Den while we talked. Both were Nox well known to me as people working hard to fit into human society.

"I guess I'm going to have to visit that auto shop and see if I can get information that the FBI couldn't. Do you remember the name of it?"

"One Stop Auto Shop, out on the southeast side of town. The kind of place you take your car when you don't trust the chain places. Or if you want to save a few bucks and don't ask questions about where the replacement parts are coming from."

31

"That sounds like it'll be a joy of a place to visit. Happen to remember the names of the two people who worked there at the time of the robbery?"

"No, but one of them was the owner. Older guy, probably about my age."

Flipping through the notepad, I found another name I had written down that morning. "I've got another possibility, if you don't mind checking it out tomorrow. Tyson Blake, went to high school with Emilio. Story I got was that they were in competing gangs, and Tyson was the sort that might want to snatch a kid for a little payback."

"Oh yeah? Which gangs?"

"Emilio was in something called La Calavera. He didn't mention which gang Tyson was in."

Ollie scrunched up his nose as he looked up at the dark ceiling. "La Calavera? Doesn't that mean The Skull, or something like that? I've never heard of a gang with that name."

"He said it was just a few of his friends in school. Sounded like they grew up and split apart after high school."

"Good for them. We need more kids to get smart and realize gangs are nothing but trouble. I'll do some searches tomorrow morning when I get in and let you know what I can find."

"Thanks, Ollie. I owe you a steak dinner for all of this information."

He nudged me with an elbow. "You don't owe me anything, Jack. Ever. I'll never repay what you did for me back then."

Talking about that first case ten years ago always made me uncomfortable, for good reason. Because the morning Ollie and I met was the day I found out my sister was dead. My hand reached up to wrap around the talisman under my shirt, and I had to force it to relax and let go.

"I'll tell Sandra you said hello," he said as he stood up from the stool. "Take care of yourself, Jack. Whatever snatched that kid could prove to be something you can't handle on your own. There have been a few too many close calls already."

After he left, my eyes were drawn back to the unknown pair at the far end of the bar. Richard was still leaning on the bar talking with them, looking around now and then to make sure he didn't need to refill drinks. I was tempted once again to call him over to ask about them, but I decided that I already had enough on my plate. Once I found Penny, or tracked down whatever had taken her, I could give in to my curiosity again. Slipping my arms into the sleeves of my coat, I waved at Richard and left to begin the long walk through the cold night to retrieve my car.

4

After a night of bad dreams, I was up early and driving through rush hour traffic to the auto shop. I'd considered going in for my normal breakfast first, but reluctantly settled for a couple of cinnamon donuts and a large cup of coffee from one of the national chains. If nothing else, it gave me something to do while sitting at stop lights for long periods waiting on the string of cars in front of me to go through.

One Stop Auto Shop was a small building constructed of concrete blocks, with three bays for vehicles. The concrete was painted blue, the garage doors red, and both looked as if they had needed a fresh coat for the last five years or more. One of the garage bays was already open, with an old Ford truck parked inside. I swung my Honda into one of the two parking spots in front of the office, and made sure to lock the doors before entering the shop.

"Good morning, how can we help you today?" the man behind the counter asked. He was pushing sixty, based on the wrinkles and thinning gray hair. The small office was covered in old auto part and tire advertisements, most ragged and dark with age. I breathed in the scent of old oil and grease as I stepped up to the counter.

"Hi, I was in here three or four years ago. I had an old clunker back then, and this nice guy worked on the engine for me. I was hoping he still worked here. I think his name was Mike."

The man's expression didn't change, but I hadn't expected it to. I was sure this guy got a lot of visits from cops and people asking questions that he didn't want to answer. "Sorry, you must be remembering the name wrong. We've never had a Mike working here."

"I'm sure that was it. He was a young guy, maybe twenty?" I thought back to the pictures I had seen on the wall of Anna's house. "A little shorter than me, maybe three or four inches. Heavyset guy, dark hair. He was such a pleasant man to deal with."

"Must have been a different shop," the man said. "But if you want to get some work done, we can help you. Engine problems with the current car, maybe?"

"I couldn't let anyone but Mike work on it after last time. It was definitely this place. I remember the blue and red, like Superman." I trotted out my friendliest smile, getting no reaction at all.

"Don't know what to tell you, fella. I've never employed anyone by that name or description."

"Really? That's too bad." So much for the nice guy approach. "But I guess I wouldn't want to admit that I employed a guy that robbed a bank with three other employees, either."

The man turned his body toward me, and placed both palms on the short counter as he leaned forward. "I don't know what it is you want here, mister, but you aren't going to get it. Now leave. I'm refusing service, as is my right."

I could feel anger from him, but nothing more than the simple human emotion. Even the Nox that are adept enough to blend in well with the human world would have trouble staying contained after being provoked. It never hurt to be sure, though.

"Maybe you don't want to admit Michael worked here for another reason. Maybe *you* were the one driving the car at the bank. Hiding the money that wasn't found when the others were arrested."

With his fists clenched, the older man came around the counter with determined steps. "You get the hell out of my shop, or I'll be calling the cops to see if you like being locked up."

Hands raised, I backed out of the grimy office. I felt confident now that there was nothing more to the old man. After a display of anger like that, even the most paranoid Nox would have given themselves away.

Returning to my car, I started the engine and pulled out of the garage's small lot. Across a potholed two-lane street was an small run down strip mall. I parked in a spot there that faced the garage, and drank the last of my coffee to stay warm. Getting comfortable in the faux leather seat, I watched the worker in the open garage bay and wished the sun weren't reflecting off the glass of the office. The glare kept me from being able to see what was going on inside.

The owner of the shop appeared after ten minutes, stepping outside the small office and holding the door open. His eyes were locked on my car, and I watched him stare at me for several minutes before he retreated back into the shop.

Soon after, Ollie sent me a text: *Sorry for the wait, here's the info.* There were two documents attached, and I opened the first labeled "Michael Castillo". There was a list of names, the four people arrested mere hours after the bank robbery. A small mugshot of each was beside the name. The two other men in the group were both older than Michael, but only by a decade or so. Last on the list was the woman who had been with them, staring into the camera with defiance and chin held high. She was only eighteen, with tattoos running around her neck and down both forearms holding up the placard with her name and arrest date. It made me wonder what kind of hard life she'd grown up in to turn bad at so young an age.

All three of the men were being held in the same unit in Huntsville, while the woman was in a female correctional facility an hour northwest of San Antonio. I wrote down her name in my notebook, a reminder that I could visit her if the auto shop stake-out didn't lead me to the possible accomplice.

Missing from the sparse file was the name of that suspected accomplice. Having worked with Ollie long enough, I knew that the file he sent me was probably all that he felt comfortable shar-ing outside of the department. The last thing he would need is someone getting hold of what he sent me and using it to accost or attack someone based on rumor or gossip.

Reading through the notes and interview transcripts, it struck me that all four of the bank robbers had been fairly con-sistent with their stories. They had discussed how easy it was to rob a bank after watching some movie on television, arguing about the best plan for days. At some point, that lighthearted discussion had turned serious, though none of them could or would say who first suggested following through. Michael did ad-mit that he felt compelled to go along with the others, but no one else mentioned coercion or the reluctance of another person to participate.

Jacqui, the young woman, had been the one to suggest taking a customer's car. All of them claimed to have thought it a genius plan to hide their identities. All of them also showed genuine surprise to hear that they had parked directly in the path of an ATM camera. The two older men brought the guns that were used, a sawn-off shotgun, a .22 caliber target rifle, and two nine millimeter pistols. Michael was adamant that the weapons had been loaded with blanks, but the other three shrugged when asked and said they'd used real bullets. No one could be sure since the weapons had never been recovered.

The four of them had been caught with nearly twenty thousand dollars, evenly split between them. When asked about the remaining fifty thousand, each of them shut their mouths and refused to talk any further. That made the feds as suspicious as it made me, and I couldn't help squinting harder at the auto shop as I thought about it. Without the missing money, I would have bought the story they peddled. That fifty thousand made me think that there was not only a fifth accomplice, but some kind of mastermind that had planned the entire thing.

I looked up to see the shop owner standing in the open doorway again, this time with a phone held up to his ear. Smiling brightly, I waved at him until he flipped me the bird and went back behind the windows that were still bouncing the sun's light directly into my eyes.

Closing the first file, I opened the second attachment and found that Ollie had sent me a copy of an arrest report for Tyson Blake. He had been picked up for minor misdemeanors half a dozen times before he was eighteen, getting a two-month stint in juvie once and let go with probation the other times. Once he turned eighteen, the arrests stopped, and his record was clean for several years. Gang Intelligence had him down as a former member of a nation-wide gang, but no one had seen him in over a year. The last known address listed in the file was his mother's house.

More than an hour had passed since I left the auto shop, and I'd only seen two other cars enter for maintenance or repairs. All three of the garage bays were occupied now, the doors up and the workers bathed in the light of the midmorning sun warming them. The placement of the business was ideal for Texas weather. Morning sunlight entered the bay doors for only a few hours each morning, preventing it from getting too hot on scorching summer days. The brick walls and metal roof would absorb some of the heat the rest of the day.

There were three employees working on the vehicles, and I wondered if the owner had been forced to downsize his workforce after the bad publicity of the bank robbery. Two of the mechanics were young men, probably just out of high school. I ruled them out as being involved right away. A third worker stuck to the shadows more often than seemed natural. I caught glimpses of a heavy black beard, but the brim of his shop cap was pulled low over his eyes. It was hard to estimate an age, but based on the way he moved I pegged him as mid-thirties at the youngest.

With my attention focused on the mechanics, I hadn't noticed a car pull up behind me. The hard knock on my window made me jump. I turned to find a large black man leaning over to glare at me through the glass. He was easily a head taller than my six feet, and looked to weigh twice as much as my two hundred pounds.

Pressing the ignition button to give the car power, I pressed another button on the door to lower the window an inch. "Can I help you?"

"You need to leave, dude." He said tersely.

"Pretty sure this is a public parking lot. Dude. I can park here until the strip mall owner tells me that I can't."

"He is." The black man shoved a sausage-like thumb in the direction of the auto shop, and I looked over to see the old man grinning smugly as he watched us through the open door. His arms were crossed, legs planted wide, and he was staring at me with visible amusement.

"That guy owns this row of stores?" I asked in disbelief.

The black guy shrugged. "Guy owns a lot of this area of town. And he said you're trespassing. So leave, before I have to make you leave. Get what I'm saying?"

My tongue pushed at the back of my teeth as I considered that new information. A lot of little pieces started to click into a better alignment in my head. I couldn't stop the grin that spread across my face. "Sure thing, Goliath. As soon as you move your car, I'll get out of here."

He stared at me for several seconds, before turning and sauntering back to his SUV. The vehicle dipped noticeably as he stuffed his large body into the driver's seat. I didn't even hear the engine start up before the SUV rolled forward enough for me to back up, explaining why I hadn't heard his arrival.

Pressing the ignition button a second time to start the engine, I reversed out of the parking spot and drove forward to exit the lot. I turned right, swerving as far as possible to get close to the auto shop. There was a faint sensation, an emanation of the chaos energy that Nox exude, but not enough for me to identify the type of creature it came from. I felt sure the bearded man was the Nox, though, since I'd ruled out the owner earlier.

I drove half-a-mile north before pulling into another parking lot. Scrolling through my Contacts list, I pressed the name I was searching for and waited patiently. The phone rang for half a minute before I heard a deep rumbling voice instruct me to leave a message.

"Nyk, it's Jack. Got a job for you today." I left details of the auto shop location and the description of the man I had seen working there. Nyk was someone I had worked with in the past. I could trust him to look into the unknown mechanic and find out his story. While not a Nox, Nyk was one of the best bounty hunters in the state because of his ability to track almost anyone or anything. He normally commanded a steep fee for his services, but we traded favors and I knew he would eventually call me to help with one of his jobs in return.

Satisfied that the Nox mechanic would soon have his secrets revealed, I decided to check out the bank that had been robbed more than three years earlier. It was far too long ago to pick up on the essence of supernatural involvement, but something about the robbery drew me in. I couldn't help but think there was more behind it than a simple spur-of-the-moment plan.

Lunch rush traffic hadn't started yet, so I was able to get through town to the bank within fifteen minutes. It was located on the first floor of a tall building, off a large street with three lanes in either direction. A car dealership took up several acres on one side of the building, and an outdoor mall was across the street. I parked in front of a busy clothing store, and walked a few hundred yards to stand on the sidewalk beside the busy street. Looking through the traffic, the bank entrance was well situated to be visible to those driving by.

The glass doors of the building opened onto a large lobby that was visible from my vantage point. I could see half a dozen chairs and couches spread out to form a couple of different seating areas. A six-foot poster board sign was set out to point customers in the direction of a branch of one of the nation's largest banks. There was a security guard standing near the entrance, watchful eyes moving constantly over the lobby. I hadn't seen any mention of a guard in the bank robbery report, so they must have decided to hire one afterwards.

I couldn't see into the small branch from across the wide street, so I walked down to the nearest crosswalk and waited patiently for the light to change. Striding quickly across to the middle traffic island and then across to the far side, I couldn't help but think that someone must have done much the same thing years before. Surely the bank had been observed and cased in advance of the robbery, regardless of the stories telling of a last-minute decision.

A car salesman called out to me as I passed the rows of gleaming new vehicles, offering me a great interest rate if I wanted to stop and take a look. Declining as politely as I could, I continued along to turn onto the cobbled parking lot in front of the towering building. There were a dozen spaces here, most reserved for bank customers. A sign directed others to the entrance of the multilevel parking garage behind the building.

Entering through the glass doors, I stopped for a moment to revel in the warmth of the lobby. The walk had left me exposed to the cold December day and sapped away all the heat I had absorbed in the car ride across town. The guard's eyes swept across me a few times as I paused there, locking on as I turned toward the bank branch. He nodded politely as I passed through into the brightly lit space.

Two modern desks were set up to my left, a few feet between them to provide a modicum of privacy for times when both were occupied with bankers and customers. To my right was an oval table with a couple of pens chained to it, a pile of deposit slips neatly stacked in a slot. I could see a small vault with safe deposit boxes behind a barred door. Ahead was the high counter with four sections set up for bank tellers. Two young women occupied the counter, chatting with each other. They turned toward me as I walked forward to stop in front of a pretty young brunette with a cute smile.

"Hi, I think I might have an old account with your bank." I laughed, trying to appear charming and forgetful at the same time. "Could you possibly look it up and find out?"

"Certainly, sir," she replied brightly, almost bouncing in her seat. "If I can see an ID, I'll run a search for your name and date of birth."

Pulling out my wallet, I swept my eyes around the edges of the ceiling. There were security camera domes all over, and I couldn't imagine there was any part of the room invisible to the system. They were a newer model, but could have easily all been in place three years ago. I slid my driver's license to the young teller, and leaned on the counter.

The bubbly girl typed happily on her keyboard, her smile not waning even a millimeter. After half a minute, she pushed my ID back across the counter. "I'm sorry, sir. Your name isn't in our system at all, even for old accounts that were closed due to inactivity."

"Well, at least I can stop wondering about it now." I shrugged and laughed. "Must have been another bank around here. Thanks for checking." Putting my wallet back in my pocket, I left the bank area and strolled around the lobby a few times. There were cameras in several places, at least two of them situated to get a view of people going in and out of the bank branch.

Pushing through the doors to exit into the cold sunlight, I plunged my hands into my coat pockets and started the walk back to my car. I couldn't find any reason for someone to decide to rob that branch, with all of the security and the minimal flow of traffic. There were several branches I had passed on my drive that were better targets and would have yielded just as much cash.

My phone pinged as I climbed back into my car, a message from Nyk that he was on the job. I knew I'd have results by the evening, or the next morning at the absolute latest. Then I'd know for sure if the Nox mechanic was involved in the bank robbery, and possibly Penny's disappearance.

5

After a quick lunch at a local Tex-Mex institution that I visited whenever I was in the northcentral part of town, I headed off to the east side. My next stop was a visit with Tyson Blake's mother. I knew I had to cross him off the list of suspects, if possible. She lived in a neighborhood that had been built in the 1960s, rows of ranch style houses set far back from the street with tall trees shading the front yards.

I left my care in front of a crumbling concrete curb, walking up three steps to a concrete path that approached the front door at the end of a sloping lawn. The grass was yellow and dormant for the winter, but looked full and cared for. I could imagine pleasant evenings for the occupants of the house cutting the grass, spreading fertilizer, or pulling the few weeds that managed to invade the yard. The spiky-leafed bushes at the front of the house were tall and trimmed into neat squares.

The screen door had heavy bars, as did the windows to either side of the door. I knocked on the wooden frame, and waited as I heard shuffling footsteps approaching. The solid door creaked open a few inches, two bright eyes staring at me from the darkness.

"Hello, I'm Jack Dahlish. I was hoping I could ask you a few questions about Tyson." I tried to give a comforting smile, holding up one of the light gray business cards that listed my private detective license number below my name and office address. I didn't need to use that stack of cards often, but humans liked the official veneer.

The door opened a few more inches, and enough light poured in to show me a small woman in her late fifties or early sixties. Her skin was wrinkled with age or too much sun, beneath snowy white hair. The hand that reached out to push the screen door open enough to grab the card was yellowed where she had been holding cigarettes between her fingers for decades. Her voice was rough from the nicotine and smoke.

"What do you want with Tyson, young man?"

"I'm just trying to rule him out of a matter I'm investigating. Do you know where I could find him? I really only have a couple of questions for him."

Her eyes narrowed, and she looked away. "I haven't seen Tyson in at least eighteen months."

"Do you know where he might have gone? Was he with someone the last time you saw him?" I kept my voice gentle, not pushing too hard with the questions. A light touch could sometimes bring answers that badgering never would.

"Why are you asking? Tell me that."

I debated with myself on how much to say, and decided to go with the truth. "A three-year-old girl was abducted from a park four days ago. Her uncle knew Tyson in high school, and they hated each other. That put him on a list of possible suspects."

"He's in Dallas," she said after a long silence. "Went with some bimbo who works in a strip club up there. Ty said he was going to be her security, but I know what that means. Boy is going to be her pimp, and probably find more girls to work for him. He called me just two nights ago, offering to send me some of his dirty money."

Cursing inwardly, I scratched Emilio's old nemesis off the list of suspects. I couldn't imagine anyone holding such a large grudge from high school that they would drive more than four hours south on the interstate just to snatch a kid from a playground.

"Thank you, ma'am. I'm glad he isn't involved."

"I hope you find that little girl. No parent should have to go through something like that."

The door creaked closed as I turned and walked down the long path back to my car. One of my two leads had just dead ended, and the other only looked half promising. I tried calling Ollie again to get his thoughts on what I'd found so far, but his phone went to voice mail after a few rings. No doubt he was dealing with his rookie.

Penny had been missing for more than four days now, and I didn't want to think about the possibility that she might already have been killed. Far too many abducted children ended up that way, but if there was a Filii Nox involved in this case then there was hope that I could still find her. For all of their failings and propensity to embrace their hatred of how humanity had treated them through the centuries, the Nox had never yet produced pedophiles.

Feeling lost, I found myself driving north as I ran my thoughts over the scant information I had about the case. Before I realized it, my car was pulling into a small gravel lot. There were no defined parking spaces, but enough room for four or five cars.

It was deserted this afternoon, and I stepped out to look at the still water of the small pond nearby.

The pond was surrounded on three sides by a thick growth of oak and mesquite trees, with brambles and tall grasses in the undergrowth. A walking trail surround the pond, one small wooden bridge going over a drainage channel that brought in water from culverts under the nearby road. I could hear the muted roar of passing cars, but they were invisible through the trees.

"What the hell am I doing here?" I asked myself, giving in to the urge to walk along the loosely packed path until I was on the far side of the pond. Once there, I stood with my hands in the deep pockets of my coat and stared at a spot several feet into the undergrowth. This was the exact spot where I had stood nearly ten years earlier, on a warm summer day. I could almost hear Ollie talking to me in a gentle voice, telling me that the body found in the trees might be my sister. The detectives and crime scene techs refused to let me get closer, and I'd had to wait for them to verify her identity at the county morgue once the body had been cut and then cleaned.

That was the day that my normal existence had ended, and I had begun a journey into the life I now led. I had been an office drone, barely getting by with small paychecks as I worked to get the experience I needed to get a better paying job with another company. At the time, my only aspirations had been a nice house in the suburbs, a sports car that would impress my friends, and enough money to take pleasant vacations to the Caribbean or Europe every summer.

My sister's murder, and the subsequent failure of the police to find the killer, had led me down a path of revenge. A strange package had led me to Lyon's Den, where I met Richard for the first time. After hearing my story, he had explained the existence of the supernatural Nox. Like anyone else, I hadn't believed his fairy tales of creatures that had adapted to hide themselves among the human masses. I left the Den angry that night, convinced the bartender had decided to have a little fun at my expense.

That strange package contained the talisman that had been around my neck every second since. It was an old coin, in excellent condition, bearing a face and writing that every historian and museum curator I had taken it to had been unable to recognize. They all tried to purchase it from me, though none could even say if the coin were thousands of years old or had been stamped out days before.

Two days later, a pair of Nox had attacked me. Their target had been the talisman, one of them trying to rip the silver chain from my neck as I fought against the other. Later, I learned that both were tengu, humanoid creatures with feathered torsos and heads. Their talon-like hands had ripped and scratched at my skin. A blaze of light filled the area, and with loud squawks and pained shrieks the creatures retreated and run away.

It was only after returning to Lyon's Den and apologizing to Richard for my previous disbelief that I learned what had happened. The talisman around my neck was a powerful Relic, imbued with the chaotic energies that had formed the universe and created the gods who had given birth to the first generations of Filii Nox. In my panic and fear, I had somehow tapped into that energy to repel the creatures.

From that day on, I had been able to sense the essences of the Nox when I opened myself to the supernatural world that was all around us. It had been that nascent ability that enabled me to eventually track down my sister's killer. Once that was done, I'd been unable to return to my boring old life and instead decided to help anyone victimized by a Nox. There were occasions when I even helped Nox to protect themselves from others within the secretive groups.

Standing at the edge of the pond, watching the water ripple as a breeze blew across the surface, I realized that I hadn't returned to this place since my sister's death. I had driven by on the road beyond the trees hundreds of times, but never once had I stopped in to stand on that graveled path.

"What would you think of me now, Jen? You were always the adventurous one, while I was stuck in a rut." I couldn't hold back a smile as I remembered my younger sister's way of poking fun at me as she was growing up. I was always the boring brother, and going out for drinks with friends was the wildest thing I'd ever done.

Thinking of my sister brought my thoughts back to Penny. Someone had taken the girl the same way someone had taken my sister, and I was determined to not let their stories end in the same way. It was time to go back to the start and find a new path to follow.

Half an hour later I was turning into the nearly full parking lot of Dawson Park. I took one of the two spaces left open, and sat in the car for several minutes listening to the ticks of the cooling engine. The playground equipment was crowded with kids, parents filling the scattered benches. The winter sun had warmed the day enough for them to venture out in light coats. A group of kids that looked to be around eight or nine were all wearing red and white baseball uniforms, practicing their hitting and catching around the small baseball diamond.

Climbing out of the car, I walked around the playground in a slow circle. My eyes were unfocused as I concentrated on the feel of the air around me. I could still faintly sense the dark essence around the slide, growing stronger or weaker as I circled the area. Taking a deep breath to steel myself, I opened my senses more than I ever usually would. The nausea and vertigo took hold almost at once.

There were faint traces of Nox presence everywhere, streaks of essence that seemed to show me movements made in the not too distant past. Hundreds, if not thousands of them filled the park. None of it was out of the ordinary for a city like San Antonio that has a Nox population in the thousands. One family regularly visiting the park could leave traces such as these over the course of many trips.

Focusing harder, I started to sift through the remnants. Most gave a hint of the wet dog smell and bristly feel that I associated with minotaurs and kishi. I knew there were large communities of both in town, with very few of them showing up on my radar over the years. Underneath those heavy layers, there was the wispy trace of something different. Something I couldn't remember ever feeling before.

I shivered as I passed through the trail of the unknown essence. My skin crawled as I felt a dry, papery sensation that made me think of old books or crackling leaves. The smell that invaded my nostrils made my lip curl in disgust, a musty odor that was familiar in a way I couldn't remember. It was entering the park from the east, growing stronger as it approached the playground.

Stopping in my slow walk, I scraped my tongue on my teeth in an attempt to remove the taste in my mouth left by the smell.

"Hey, mister!" a shrill voice yelled out, shaking me out of my sensory overload. A short woman with a tight ponytail and angry eyes was standing inches away, her face jutted forward as she yelled at me. "What the hell is wrong with you? Are you some kind of pervert?"

Looking around, I realized that I was standing on the shredded rubber surface in the middle of the playground. Most of the kids were still running around, unaware of anything but their own fun. A few were looking at me, though I felt they were more scared or curious about the fact that the woman was yelling at me.

A hard poke in my chest made me turn back to the angry little ball of fury. "I called the cops on your pervert ass." A bright light flashed in my eyes as her phone appeared and she snapped a picture of me. "And now they'll know what you look like."

"Look, lady, I'm working. Okay? I couldn't care less about your ankle-biters." Immediately, I regretted the words as I saw her eyes go wide and her mouth grow smaller. "Ah, forget it. I'm going."

"Yeah, you better run, perv!" She kept shouting at me as I strode toward my car, hunching down to hide in the depths of my herringbone coat. Trying to ignore her, and the glares from every other adult around the park, I forced myself to revisit the smell and feel of the last essence I had detected. It was definitely a Nox of some sort, but one that I'd never encountered before.

Approaching my car, I found a beautiful redhead leaning on the Honda's hood. A long red coat covered her from chin to knees, wrapped tightly around her body. Her slim shapely legs were crossed at the ankles, leaving her weight balanced on a single three-inch stiletto heel. For as long as I live, I'll never be able to understand how women do that. Or why they put themselves through the pained feet that come of it.

She pushed herself to a standing position as I got closer, red lips cocked up on one side with mirth as her eyes looked from me to the angry parents and back again. "Well, you certainly know how to make an impression, Mr. Dahlish."

"Usually it's a good impression," I muttered, coming to a stop a few feet away. Squinting, I tried to remember where I had seen the woman before. "You're that reporter, aren't you?"

A dazzling smile met my words, and she stood a little straighter. In the heels, she was almost as tall as I was. "Karen Kilgraff, KRSA News."

"Uh huh," I said, feeling bad as she slightly deflated at my simple response. "What brings you to the park? And more specifically, my car?"

"Good sources are the hallmark of an excellent reporter, Mr. Dahlish. I have great ones, and they tell me that you've been hired by the family to investigate the disappearance of Penny Castillo."

"Well, Karen, it was nice to meet you." Walking around her, I pulled my keys from my pocket and pressed the button to unlock the doors. The last thing I needed was to have a reporter taking any kind of interest in me.

"Jack. You don't mind if I call you Jack, do you? I'm not here to get in your way or pester you to find out what you might have found that the police couldn't." She shimmied to stand between me and the door as she spoke. "You saw my reports about the other child abductions, didn't you?"

The words took me aback. "Abductions? Plural? I saw one video where you talked about a kid going missing in October."

"That was only the tip of the iceberg. There has been a string of incidents, at least seven that I've been able to find in the last several months. Eight, with little Penny." Karen looked over at the angry mothers, still glaring in my direction and seemingly closer than they had been the last time I glanced over. "Look, can we go somewhere and talk? I'll share everything I know, if you'll do the same. Maybe together we can fit some pieces together."

It was tempting to just walk away. After all, why should other abductions have anything to do with the case I was working on? I was after a Nox obviously bent on harming at least one human, not trying to track down human deviants.

Who was I kidding? I had as soft a heart as the next guy, and I had to listen on the off chance that the abductions were all connected in some way. Plus, those greenish hazel eyes were making me want to do whatever it took to keep the beautiful reporter around me for a while longer.

"You know the Pig Stand?"

"I've lived in San Antonio for many years, Jack. Of course I do."

"Let's head over there. I can use some hot coffee while we talk." I admired the view as she turned to walk across the lot to a small red sports car. The woman was obsessed with the color, but she looked great in it, so I wasn't going to complain.

6

S itting in a booth near the fogged up window, Karen ignored her cup of steaming coffee. I had my hands cradled around my own warm cup, trying to defrost fingers that had started to go numb after standing out in the cold park for too long.

"I've heard stories about you," she said with a faint smile.

"About me? Those must have been boring stories."

"Far from it. Those two kids that were ripped apart out at UTSA a few years ago? I heard from a source that *you* were the one to find the killer. They were never arrested, but the killings stopped after that week."

I shrugged uncomfortably, sipping the coffee and letting my eyes roam around the nearly empty diner. "Sounds like the kind of story people come up with to explain something that they can't understand. Not sure why they had to pull me into it."

I remembered the case well, of course. The first kid, a college freshman, had been found eviscerated on the campus grounds by late night partiers on a Saturday. Ollie called me in right away, a gut feeling telling him it might be one of mine. Seeing the body, ripped apart with blood spatters stretching out for ten feet or more, I'd known he was right.

The second body was found two nights later, a professor who had just started her first year at the college. The body was found in the same condition, and I called in Nyk to help me track down the killer. Both of us had known it was the work of a werewolf, especially when the hearts and livers weren't found with the bodies. When a werewolf gives in to the killing urge, those are the organs they choose to eat first.

The very next night, we found the rabid werewolf. It was an old man, tired of fighting the urges he had suppressed for more than seventy years. He was stalking another student when Nyk tracked him down, and together we put an end to the threat. Turning him over to the police wasn't an option, since there was no physical evidence that could tie him to the crimes. He would be back on the streets in a few days, killing faster and faster as the blood frenzy took hold. We put him down, as quickly and painlessly as possible.

"So, missing kids?" I prompted, starting to feel uncomfortable under her silent gaze.

Her smirk clearly said she would let me drop the subject for now, but that it wouldn't be forgotten. "Which report did you see from October?"

"There was more than one? It was a four-year-old, last seen on the swings."

She nodded. "Fiona Griffith. She was the second child taken that month, and as far as I know she still hasn't been found. The first child disappeared from another park south of town. The father saw her climbing on the geodesic dome, that thing with bars that form triangles. He looked away for a few seconds, and when he turned back his four-year-old daughter was gone. Disappeared, and none of the other kids claim to have seen it happen."

"That's awful. Both are still missing?"

"They are. The police have no leads at all. No evidence at the site of either disappearance, no witnesses who saw anything out of the ordinary, and every person they've taken in for questioning either has an alibi or were ruled out by searches of homes and vehicles."

"It's sad, but how does two kids taken from parks in October relate to Penny being taken from a park in December?"

"Because it's not just two kids in October, Jack. There was one taken late in September, three in November, and Penny is the second this month. Eight children missing, all from different parks around the city, all disappearing without anyone seeing them taken."

I frowned at that, wondering how I could have missed such a cluster of odd occurrences. "All from a park, and never more than one from the same park?"

Karen nodded in confirmation. "That's why it doesn't make sense. Child abductors are usually either estranged parents or pedophiles. Eight of them rules out parent involvement, and pedophiles by and large stick to their normal hunting ground. They don't go all over the city hoping to find a random kid they can steal away without being seen."

"I can think of a few serial killers who have done that sort of thing," I said. "There was a guy in Germany back in the sixties and seventies that would take a train to nearby villages and towns to kill women and girls."

Karen waved that away. "I'll grant you that there have been rare cases. But those are the exceptions to the rule. Plus, if this were a serial killer the police would have found at least one body by now. The parks where the first five abductions happened were combed for days, and I know some officers who still go back and walk the grounds on their days off."

Draining my cup and waving for a refill, I thought about the new information. Eight children, eight different parks. "Were all of them girls? What ages?"

"All girls," she confirmed. "Three and four years old, though the fourth child taken was five. She looked small for her age, though." The waitress raised an eyebrow as she heard the last comments while refilling my coffee. I wondered what kind of gossip would be fueled in the kitchen.

"Can you get me the information on the abductions? Especially the names of the parks, the part of the park the kids were last seen, and the dates."

Leaning back against the padded plastic of the booth seat, she stared at me for a few seconds. I could see the mental calculations running in her head, the reporter inside of her wanting to trade the information for something else while the moral part of her wanted to just give me the info in the hopes I could succeed where three months of police investigations had failed.

"Give me your e-mail," she said finally, glancing at an expensive rose gold watch strapped around a creamy pale wrist. "I have to be at the station to start prepping for the five o'clock, and then I'm anchoring the ten o'clock tonight. I can send you the information you want as soon as I get a chance. I'll try to include my reports, and pull the first few that were covered by one of our junior reporters before I got involved."

I pulled out one of my white cards, the ones with nothing more than my name and office phone number on it. Karen was already holding out a slim red pen, which I took with a grin. "Is everything you wear red?" I asked jokingly as I carefully wrote out each letter of my e-mail address, trying to keep it legible.

"Play your cards right, and someday you may get to find out." I jerked my head up at that comment, to find a mischievous smile on her face. She grabbed the pen and card from my slack hands, tucking them away in a pocket inside her red coat.

Still dumbstruck, I could only watch as she slid out of the booth and walked out of the diner with her hips swaying seductively. Karen even managed to make getting into her car look sexy, even though I could only partially see her through the fogged windows.

"Get your mind out of the gutter, Dahlish," I muttered to myself, turning to see the waitress smirking at me from behind the counter. Smiling sheepishly, I gulped dawn the warm coffee. Leaving money on the table, I buttoned up my coat and exited the warmth of the diner to stride across the cold parking lot to my Honda.

It was past midafternoon, and if all the child abductions proved to be connected then my job had just gotten harder. On the positive side, I would also have more angles to work it from. Pulling out my phone, I started to do a search for the story I remembered seeing the day before so I could get the name of the park.

A popping bubble sound and blue light around the screen of the phone told me I had just received a text message. Switching over to my texts, I found a message from Nyk. He already had results, and wanted me to call him as soon as I could.

Starting my car so that I could connect to the Bluetooth system, I scrolled through my recent calls list and pressed the number I'd called earlier in the morning. The phone rang only once before a growling voice answered.

"What?"

"Nyk, it's Jack."

"Oh. You ready for this?"

"Yeah." That's why I called, I resisted adding.

"Guy at the auto shop is a were-beaver. Can you believe that?"

"A were what? I've never even heard of such a thing."

Nyk laughed, a rumbling sound that made me think of boulders falling down a mountainside. "Incredibly rare. I've come across them only once before. I didn't ask their origin, because frankly I don't want to know."

"Yeah, I'm with you on that. So does he look good for being part of the bank robbery?"

"Oh, definitely. He fessed up to that as soon as he saw me. Been carrying it on his conscience for years, I'd bet. Even told me how the shop owner had planned it out and then coerced the few who weren't willing to go along. The money the cops didn't recover was funneled through accounts to help buy more property, though Chuck didn't know specifics on that."

"The were-beaver's name is Chuck? Can this get any weirder?" I had to let out a few chuckles of my own. "What about the disappearance? Does he know anything about that?"

"Nah, he didn't even know that Castillo had a family. Sounds like your guy was wary about talking personal stuff at work."

"The shop owner is still a viable suspect," I said. "He could have known about the family, or had one of his goons find out." Thinking back to the hulking black guy that had shooed me away from the parking lot earlier in the day, I couldn't really imagine him being the type of person capable of that kind of investigation. Or a subtle kidnapping from a park.

"Maybe. I don't see it. That guy is pure human, fueled by greed. I don't think he'd be afraid of anyone trying to tie him to the robbery after all this time. Any evidence of that missing cash disappeared through a dozen layers of offshore accounts and shell companies, by my guess."

Sighing, I rubbed a hand through my hair. "Yeah, he didn't give off a 'kidnap the kid to keep a guy silent' vibe when I met him. More like a wannabe mob boss, on a very small scale." It looked like that line of inquiry had gone nowhere, just like Emilio's old high school rival. Especially with the information of more child abductions that could be related. "Thanks for helping on that, Nyk. It looks like I can drop those guys from my investigation."

"No problem. I got a thing I might call you in on this weekend or next. Big bounty."

"Call me. I still owe you one for that thing last month, too."

Ending the call, I switched back to the news story and found the name of the park. It was way out on the far west side of San Antonio, a part of town that had been expanding rapidly for the last half decade. People who used to enjoy rural living close to the second largest city in the state were now encircled by subdivisions and strip malls. Many had no doubt sold out at astronomical prices to developers who could shove five or six houses onto their acre of land.

I would have to suffer through rush hour traffic on the way back, but I knew I needed to go check out that park. If I could find a trace of the same dry, papery essence I had felt at Dawson

Park, then it would almost guarantee the abductions were related. I didn't hold out much hope of it, though. The traces of taste and smell had been faint at Dawson after four days, and it had been two months since the October kidnapping of Fiona Griffith.

While driving across town, I tried calling Ollie again to see if he had any information on the other kidnappings. His phone went right to voice mail, and I left a rambling message that no doubt sounded more like someone stringing five thoughts into one sentence. He would call me back later, though. Ollie only turned his phone off when working an active accident or crime scene.

Driving past the purple and yellow towering structure of a Sea World roller coaster, I felt a little surprised at how the city had grown. When I was a kid, you had to practically drive into the sticks to reach the aquatic park. Now there were office buildings, apartments, and restaurants all over the place. The road was even a highway with exits instead of a string of stoplights with intersections. There was nothing like thinking about how things used to look to make me feel old.

The park was near a very busy intersection half-a-mile north of the outer loop, 1604. At nearly five o'clock on a Wednesday afternoon, it was full of kids kicking around a ball for soccer practice. There was still a week left before the schools started the long holiday break, a few months before the soccer season really started, and the coaches were already putting pre-teens through their paces. That was serious dedication to the most amateur of amateur sports.

There was no large playground at this park, just a large soccer field, baseball field, and pavilion where people could get out of the rain or hold barbecues. Smaller kids were running around on the grass while their older siblings were in soccer practice. A small swing set had been erected nearby, along with several bars at varying heights that I could imagine kids hanging from and laughing wildly.

Karen's report had mentioned the swings, so I made my way over as casually as possible. The last thing I needed was a repeat of the events at Dawson Park earlier in the afternoon. Luckily, there were no kids currently swinging, so I wouldn't draw as much attention while I loitered there. Keeping my face toward the soccer field so that any casual observer would think I was watching the practice, I breathed deeply and prepared to open my senses to the full depths of the world around me.

The first thing I felt was the earthy putrescence of vampires. A family of them based on the strength of the moist dirt smell that filled my nose. I filed that information away to look into later, since I had been unaware of a new clutch in town. I would need to make sure they were adhering to the Covenants that kept the many varieties of Nox from preying on unwilling humans.

It was hard to push aside the vampiric essences, and it required my full concentration to look deeper. There were older traces of minor creatures, the weaker varieties that lurk around the edges of civilization. They would have fled rapidly when the vampire clutch moved into the area, rivalries between different types of Nox sometimes more dangerous than outright attacks on humans.

I was on the verge of closing myself off, ending the nausea and vertigo, when a faint whiff of the musty odor bloomed and then faded away behind the moist earth smell. The cloying taste filled my mouth again, and I retched as I closed my senses to the essences. Whatever creature had taken Penny had definitely visited this park, as well. That taste in my mouth was all I needed for confirmation.

There was no way to know when the creature had visited, or even be sure it had a hand in the disappearance of Fiona. The coincidence was too strong to be chance, however. I felt a faint niggling of familiarity with the odor I had picked up from the essence, and it was killing me that my mind couldn't connect the dots and fill in the memory. Trying to force it was making it feel even farther away.

Looking around the park, I was happy to see that at least this time no one had taken notice of me. Well, almost no one. A woman on the far side of the soccer field had her head turned in my direction, away from where the kids were practicing kicking a ball into the net. She was standing behind a group of other parents, and I could only see dark hair framing a pale face. Her gaze seemed almost too intense, though I couldn't even make out the color of her eyes.

"Probably just a mother picking up on someone who doesn't belong," I assured myself, hunching into my knee length coat and walking back to my car. I would check out more of the parks tomorrow, once I had the information from Karen, but for now there was one place I felt sure I could get a nudge in the right direction. I just had to fight through rush hour traffic to get there.

At least it would be time for dinner when I arrived.

7

It was already dark by the time I parked my car at the office and started to walk toward the Riverwalk. Night always came early in winter, which one would think should lead to increased work for someone like me. The Nox were born of the night, after all, and felt more comfortable in it. Those that turned against the Covenants and started to unleash pent-up hatreds and frustration on humans tended to do so in the darkness. Oddly, though, winter was always a quieter time of year, and two thirds of my work was in the warmer summer months when nights were shorter.

Several people I'd worked with through the years had theories to explain that. One guy, a half-giant, had said that he felt restless during the summers. The long hours of daylight when he would have preferred to be at home and away from the crush of humanity made him feel stir crazy by the time the darkness came and he felt at ease leaving to sample whatever entertainments he could find. Which were many in his case, after a decade of high-paying contracts coming off the bench for several NBA teams. A seven foot guy that was pure muscle made an attractive prospect, especially when he was consistently one of the better defenders in the league. Being slower than the purely human players had been a drawback, however, since he scored less often and took longer to get back to the opposite end of the court.

Pushing into the dark interior of the Den, I was shocked to find the place full of patrons. All of them had dropped the shapeshifted disguises that made them look human, as well, which told me that a ward had been placed around the bar to prevent any normal humans from deciding to drop in for the night. It was something that Richard did a few times a month, to provide a safe place for Nox to gather and enjoy themselves without restraint.

Heads turned to look at me as I stood just inside the doorway. As one of only two humans in the place, I stood out. The fact that I carried the talisman that made me a kind of policeman of the supernatural world made me unwelcome. Few of the Nox in the San Antonio area were unaware of me after all this time, though there were many of them I had never met or had reason to encounter. People who carried one of the Nine, as the talismans were called for obvious reasons, were almost like infamous celebrities in the Nox world. Information about them spread like wildfire when a new person took on the role.

Richard sauntered over and waved me toward a dark corner of the bar. "Jack, it's not a good night. Come back tomorrow?" Richard had long been accepted among the creatures of the Nox. He carried another of the rare chaos-infused Relics, though one with vastly different qualities from my talisman. In the ten years I'd known him, he'd never even mentioned what his Relic was. I'd picked up the sense of it whenever we were close, but politeness kept me from asking about it.

"Not a problem. I just have a quick question for you. I'm hoping you can point me in the right direction for some information." I described to him the feel and smell of the essence I had detected at both parks. Richard had no experience with the senses granted by my talisman, but he had been around for a long time and known a handful of talisman bearers who had lived in or passed through the city.

He gave me a look after I finished talking, a look that warned me that I wasn't going to like what he was about to say. "Don't say it," I told him. "Do not tell me I need to go see..."

"Selma," he said joyfully. "You know she's the best person to talk to, Jack." He eyed me up and down, examining the expensive herringbone coat that I had blown an entire retainer check to buy a few years before. "I'd change before I go down there, though."

"Yeah, yeah." I grumbled. Looking around the bar, I saw a handful of familiar faces. Terrance was sitting on the same stool as the night before, the greenish cast of his goblin skin on full display this time. Warts and all. "I'll get out of here so everyone can relax again. Put a round of drinks on my tab."

"Your tab is already long enough to buy me a new car," Richard called as I left with a wave. A large part of me felt sad that I couldn't mingle with the crowd of Nox, get to know some of them better. Having the coin around my neck would always set me apart, and make me an object of fear or disgust among most of the supernatural creatures.

As a consolation, I got to go visit Selma. It had been four years since the last time I saw the old crone, and I would have been quite happy to go forty more without seeing her. Walking back to my car, I reflected that it was a good thing I hadn't been able to grab dinner at the Den as intended.

I made the short drive to my small house, a purchase I had made nine years ago when the housing market was at the bottom of the crash. An early successful case had netted me a large fee, enough for a down payment on the old home that had been in serious need of some TLC. I'd like to say that in the intervening years I had worked hard to renovate rooms and turn my home into a shining example for the neighborhood. But the reality was that I spent far more time in my office or driving around town, and usually returned home just long enough for a few hours of sleep and a shower.

The narrow yard was neat and tidy, thanks to a neighbor who loved gardening and had been ecstatic when I told her she could do whatever she wanted with my yard. Azalea bushes lined the short path from the sidewalk to my faded front door, looking a bit dull in the winter but providing a burst of color in spring. Two tall oak trees towered over them, one to either side of the walkway. Along the short driveway leading to the carport where I parked my car was a selection of flowering plants that required a lot of care and would die in seconds if the old dear next door ever moved away.

The neighborhood was in the process of gentrification, a term I had never liked and really wasn't sure I enjoyed being a part of. Run-down homes that had once hosted rusted old cars in the front yards and rotating casts of druggies were now being snapped up at outrageous prices by hipster yuppies. They turned the houses into postcard perfection, making the rest of us look like awful neighbors by comparison. I had often thought of selling for a price that would be almost half again what I bought it for even without any improvements, but I liked being close to work and central to every other part of town.

Inside the house, I tossed my keys onto a small table by the door. There was a row of coat hooks opposite the door, where I put my gray herringbone after taking it off. The walls had received a fresh coat of off-white paint soon after I moved in, but been untouched since. Under my feet were original wood floors, badly in need of sanding and a new coat of varnish to protect them.

Passing through a small living room with nothing more than a couch and a tv, I stopped in my tiny kitchen to root around in the cabinets. There were several cans of beans that I couldn't remember buying, an opened bag half full of pasta shells, a sleeve of stale crackers, and a can of tuna. The small fridge, purchased to be a stop gap until I renovated the kitchen and got something bigger and fancier, had a half gallon of milk nearing expiration and some bottles of water.

Spreading the tuna across the crackers provided something that resembled a meal. One that I enjoyed more than I had most sit-down dinners, being honest. After washing it down with a glass of milk, I stepped into my bedroom at the back of the house. There was a second bedroom in the front of the house that I had set up as a home office, with a small daybed for visitors. So far it had gone unused.

I pulled off my shirt and jeans, rooting around in the basket of dirty clothes for something else to put on. The place I was headed was not the sort of area where you wanted to be seen as someone with the money or time to be clean. That would only single me out as a mark. I found a pair of nylon workout pants that had been soaked in sweat after a rare jog around the neighborhood two weekends before, and a shirt that I had worn three times before deciding I couldn't pretend it was clean enough to wear again. Both also had the stale smell that soaks into worn clothing in the laundry basket.

An old coat in the back of my closet went on next, a mostly cotton hoodie with holes in the pockets and fraying at the elbows. I also found a pair of shoes I had replaced after a couple of years of constant wear and then never thrown away. "Just in case" turned out to be this one time eighteen months later. Opening a drawer, I pulled out a pair of gloves and an orange and yellow beanie with earflaps. Humming "The Hero of Canton", I grabbed my keys and drove away from the increasingly nice neighborhood.

Back downtown, I parked in the lot across the street from my office and stepped out into the cold night air. The forecast had called for low forties overnight, and it certainly felt as if it were already that chilly. The gloves and beanie kept all but my face covered, and I stuck my hands in the threadbare pockets of the old hoodie as I walked in the opposite direction from La Villita.

Half a mile west of my office, I-10 cut through downtown. The overpasses created pockets of covered concrete that were protected enough for homeless people to set up their tarp tents or cardboard box homes. I twisted through shopping carts heaped with junk and precious treasures, moving through the small camp to two barrels at the center lit with burning newspaper and wood scraps. Ingeniously, the homeless camp had been erected in such a way to shield the light from being seen by the cars passing a hundred feet away. In the darkness underneath the interstate, only the most observant or paranoid would spot the couple of dozen tents and boxes.

Continuing through the camp, ignoring hostile glares, I passed between two tarpaulin tents and had to duck down as the concrete at my feet continued to rise to meet the hard deck of the interstate above. The constant buzzing of tires passing overhead was enough to drown out my thoughts as it echoed in the tight space.

Soon I was on my hands and knees, crawling forward. The rough concrete was scraping my knees and palms through clothing, and my back was rubbing against the bottom of the roadway above me. I crawled for several minutes, longer than it should have been possible to keep moving forward, until the space before me began to open up.

Anyone who stumbled onto this place would assume that they had gotten turned around in the tight confines and ended up right back where they began. The same tarps and cardboard boxes were arrayed before me, two burning barrels in the center. However, there were no people here. There was no noise of cars passing over my head. This place was still and silent, like a tomb.

"Well, well," a dry voice hissed out. "Jack Dahlish, come to visit the crone once again." A figure shambled out from behind one of the tents, wrapped in shadows so that I could only make out stringy hair and wrinkled skin. The figure was very short, several inches short of five feet, hunched over and walking as if one leg refused to cooperate.

"Selma," I said in greeting, stepping forward to meet her near one of the barrels. The light from within turned a sickly green as she got closer, providing no heat at all.

"You come to seek my wisdom," she stated firmly. Many thought of the old woman as nothing more than a simple witch, but I knew the truth. She was a strigoi, an old Romany woman who had died at least two hundred years before and risen from the grave with abilities similar to a vampire. No one knew what went into creating the strigoi, creatures entirely separate from the chaos-energy-created Nox. I couldn't even sense her essence the one time I had attempted it in her presence. Instead, I had felt an absolute sensory void, a sensation that had left me shaking and puking when I dragged myself out of it.

"I do. There are children going missing, and I can't identify what is taking them. I'm hoping that you can share your wisdom with me." Always a good policy to be humble when requesting help from a creature that you're fairly confident is more powerful than you are.

"You mean Richard sent you," Selma said with a hoarse laugh before her tone turned serious. "You know the price of my help. Are you willing to pay?"

This was the thing that really made me dread any visit to the shadow realm the strigoi inhabited. The reason I still had nightmares of my last visit, dreams that would jerk me awake covered in sweat and often lying on the floor with my pillow and sheets strewn around the room. Swallowing the lump in my throat I nodded and sat heavily on the ground.

Selma reached out a lumpy gray hand, the smell of putrefied flesh filling my nostrils as she got closer. The cold and clammy appendage latched onto the side of my head, working under the beanie so she could touch my skin. Closing my eyes, I braced myself for what was to come.

Strigoi feed off human emotions, the stronger the better. They can only touch the worst emotions, though. Anger, fear, despair, sadness. To bring all of these emotions to the surface, they could burrow into your mind and force you to relive your worst memories. Last time, I had managed to satisfy her with the anger and sadness from the day my parents had died. I didn't count on getting off that easily again.

I tried to conjure up memories of being dumped by old girl-friends, hoping the pain of those experiences would satisfy her hunger. To add to the mix, I remembered the absolute rage I had felt when a good friend in college had been sleeping with the girl I'd been dating for more than a year. It was the kind of memory that I hated to dwell on.

None of it was enough for the strigoi. The threads of her hunger spread farther and faster, memories stuttering through my head like someone flipping through a stack of old Polaroids. Deep down, I had always known where it would end. It was the one memory I didn't want to relive, even less than the one I had been reliving earlier in the day.

A face flashed behind my eyes, a smiling young woman. Freckles spread liberally across her cheeks and nose, the faint beginnings of wrinkles around her eyes and mouth from frequent smiles and laughter. Purple hair falling to her shoulders, bangs almost covering her hazel eyes. A face that was so different from my own, and yet so alike. My sister, Jen.

8

It was a sunny day in late April. I had just started my first post-college job, data entry and manning a customer complaint line for a local bank. After two years of studying not much of anything, I'd decided that my future was in finance. Never mind that the world was in the midst of the largest recession in decades. It was 2010, I was twenty four years old, and my future was bright.

My parents died six years earlier, leaving me to care for my sister. Jennifer was five years younger, a precocious new teenager mourning the greatest loss of her life. I had done my best, working two and three jobs when I could find them to support both of us. Delaying college had seemed like the right thing to do, and I started my classes the same year Jen was a senior in high school.

By the time I was starting on the path to becoming the high-powered stockbroker of my dreams, my sister was nearing the end of her first year at San Antonio College. We perhaps didn't talk as much as we should have, sharing a tiny one-bedroom apartment. I slept on the couch while she had the bedroom as her private space, but I was in and out for short bits between jobs and hanging out with friends when there were a few extra bucks to spend.

Wednesday afternoon, my second week in the new job, I stumbled into the apartment exhausted but wanting to head out to meet a couple of college friends at a new club opening downtown. Tossing the keys of my parent's old car on the formica countertop, I started pulling off my tie and unbuttoning the restrictive dress shirt.

"Jack, that you?"

"No, Jen. I'm the other person who shares this shitty apartment with you. Oh, wait. There's only you and me." I didn't say I was nice back then. My frustrations came out a lot more than they should have, often at my sister's expense.

"Sor-ree," she called, stretching the word to two syllables. The bedroom door swung open, and she leaned on the doorframe to stare at me. Her light brown hair had been dyed purple a few months before, triggering nights of arguments and yelling between us. Whatever boyfriend she'd been hanging around with at the time had talked her into it, and then my disapproval convinced her to keep it. "Do you have a second to talk about something?"

Groaning, I started to pull off the one pair of nice slacks that I owned. "Do we have to do it now? I'm supposed to meet the guys at seven, and it's going to take forever to get down there in this traffic."

"It's important, Jack." I looked up to see her biting on her lower lip, arms crossed over her chest. In hindsight, I knew that those were signs of distress. Especially for my sister, who could smile and laugh even while I was raging about purple hair or a belly button piercing.

Unfortunately, back then I'd been far too wrapped up in myself to notice. "Later, Jen. I just spent nine hours at work, and I want to get out and relax a little." Retreating into the small bathroom, I closed the door and forgot all about my sister as I stood under the cold water in the shower.

After becoming a surrogate parent, I started to resent my sister within a few years. In my immature mind, it was always her fault I had to work multiple jobs just to pay the bills. When I had to turn down weekend trips out of town with old friends, I always blamed Jennifer for holding me back from living my life. And when the longest relationship I'd ever had ended, I raged at my sister for being the reason my girlfriend had looked to my friend for the passion I didn't have time to give her.

In short, I was a self-obsessed prick.

Showered and dressed in casual clothing, I left the bathroom to find the bedroom door closed. Loud music was coming from inside, the kind of pounding angry tones that let you know it was hard-core metal. Yet another thing my sister picked up from her succession of loser boyfriends. Shaking my head in disgust, I grabbed my keys and put my hand on the doorknob.

Hesitating, I turned back and knocked on the bedroom door. After a few seconds of no response, I knocked harder. The volume of the music dropped slightly. "What?" From her tone, I could tell Jen was in a super sulk.

"I'll be back around midnight," I said. "We can talk in the morning, before I head to work."

"Yeah. Whatever." The music volume was cranked up even higher than before, her signal that she was done with the conversation.

Shrugging, convinced that whatever she was upset about could wait, I left the apartment and enjoyed a night nursing the one drink I could afford while my friends got totally smashed. In the end, I had to drive them both back to their apartment near the UTSA campus up north. It was almost two by the time I got home, and I dropped onto the couch without even taking my shoes off.

My cheap alarm clock started blaring at 5:30, waking me from dreams of wealth and privilege. Rubbing at sandpapery eyes, I shuffled into the bathroom to throw water on my face and quickly shave. As I scraped the razor over my skin, I stared into my red sleep-deprived eyes and promised to stop neglecting my needs. For only the ten thousandth time.

As soon as I was dressed and presentable, I popped a couple of frozen waffles in the toaster and knocked on the bedroom door to wake my sister. Returning to the kitchen, I poured syrup on the waffles and ate quickly. When Jen still hadn't left her bedroom by the time I finished breakfast, I knocked on the door again.

"Jen, don't be late to class. I have to get to work, so we'll talk tonight. Okay?"

There was no response, and I shrugged. I felt sure that she was still mad and giving me the silent treatment in revenge. Leaving the apartment, I didn't think twice about it. All through that long day at work, typing furiously and apologizing profusely to angry customers over the phone, I never thought once about my sister. I never wondered what had been so important that she wanted to discuss it with me the night before.

Entering the apartment that evening, I found it just as I had left it in the morning. My syrup-sticky plate was still in the sink, the kitchen light turned on while the rest of the apartment was dark. Clothes I had pulled off upon waking were still scattered around the floor. The bedroom door was still closed.

For the first time, I felt a faint stirring of worry. Jen was the neat freak of the family, the one who always did dishes before leaving the apartment or put my dirty clothes into the laundry basket. Even when we were in the middle of explosive arguments she would clean up after me, more for her own peace of mind than because she felt I deserved it. Finding the place still a mess was triggering alarm bells in my head.

Crossing to the bedroom door, I knocked gently. "Jen? Is everything okay?" I waited, my head close to the door as I listened for any movement or reply. Hearing nothing after several seconds, I knocked and called out louder. "Jen? You there?"

When there was no answer again, I twisted the doorknob and grunted in surprise when it turned freely. As soon as she turned sixteen, Jen had started locking her door even when she wasn't in the room. It was her way of ensuring a private place to escape the world beyond. She'd even dragged me out to Home Depot to buy a new doorknob, one that needed a real key instead of being easily unlocked by a nail file or thin screwdriver.

Swinging the door open, I glimpsed a room that I had only seen small portions of for the last three years. Her small twin bed was neatly made, the pink and purple sheets tightly tucked in under the mattress. A folding table was set up in one corner, holding an old computer we had managed to buy secondhand from one of her classmates. Scratched and worn, her six drawer dresser was against the nearest wall, a plain mirror hung over it. The only new thing we owned, a large stereo, was on top of the dresser with a stack of CD's beside it. The wall over the bed was covered in pictures torn from old magazines, hunky celebrities and models that she had tried to copy the looks of.

The floor of the room was immaculate, the carpet clean and thick under my feet. I walked into the room and stood there looking around at the meager possessions, feeling for the first time that I should have shown my sister more love and affection through the years. The sliding closet door was not fully closed, and I stepped over to pull it back. Jen's closet was the only cluttered area of her room, with stuffed animals from her childhood on the shelf over my head and old shoes scattered around the floor. The hangers on the short bar were all empty.

Feeling panicked now, I crossed to pull open the drawers in the dresser. Her underwear, bras, and socks were gone. Some old things had been left behind, the torn and unwearable stuff that poor people find it hard to let go of. I stood in open-mouthed shock, staring at the mostly empty drawers for several minutes.

Too late, I chastised myself for not taking five minutes to listen to her the night before. Was this what she was trying to tell me? That she was leaving? Or was there something else, some problem that she was facing that forced her to flee in an effort to get away from it? I looked around the room in despair as the questions chased themselves around my brain.

That's when I saw the note. It was on a piece of purple paper, blending in almost perfectly with the sheets. Grabbing it up, I read the short note in growing surprise.

Jack, I'm leaving. I tried to tell you, to explain why. But you didn't have time for me, like always. I appreciate what you've done for me since mom and dad died, but now I have to make my own life. There are some people I know that offered me a job. The money is good. Don't try to find me. I'll call when I'm ready to talk. Jen.

Sinking down to sit on the bed, I read the note over and over. I had no idea who my sister's friends were, no clue what kind of people she hung around with or what job they might have to offer her. My first thought was drugs. The hair, the piercings, the loud metal music. It all fit the idea that she had fallen in with a crowd that used and probably sold drugs. And I had been such a bad brother that she thought it preferable to be with them than to stay with me.

I cried then. For the first time in six years, I put my head in my hands and I cried. It took her leaving for me to realize how much I loved my sister. For me to realize how much of a selfish jerk I'd been over the years, increasingly so as I focused on my dreams of a lucrative career. Effectively, I'd pushed Jen away by starving her need for love and affection.

That night, I spent hours searching her room. It took several dozen guesses to find the password for her computer. *Jackson*, my full first name, was the password that kept her secrets safe. That was a dagger right through my heart, to see how much she loved me even as I had increasingly ignored her.

Jen had been too smart, more than I ever was. Her old emails had been deleted, so that I found nothing but spam and a few old draft emails where she'd started to express her unhappiness with her life. I didn't know who those emails were meant for, but couldn't help but wish she had sent at least one of them to me. Perhaps she could have gotten through to me electronically.

Cycling through the pictures that Jen had stored on her computer, I found mostly old photos of our parents. Some showed Jen and I as young kids, smiling and laughing at whatever we were doing when the picture was taken. I only had memories of a few of them, which made me feel even more depressed.

By midnight, I gave up on the search. If there was anything in her room that would tell me where she had gone or who she had been hanging around with, I couldn't find it. Leaving the bedroom, I closed the door behind me and slumped down on the couch. There were no options that I could see, other than waiting for Jen to come back or reach out to me. She was nineteen, and the police wouldn't bother looking for someone who had obviously left of their own free will.

The memory started to fade, and I felt the tendrils of the strigoi pulling back. Her hand against my head no longer felt cold and clammy. Now it was warm and soft, and I almost moaned in disappointment as it was pulled away.

Opening my eyes, I was looking at a woman who appeared no older than fifty. Warm, healthy skin with a vitality and glow that most women would jealously covet. Selma's eyes were the only thing that gave away her true self, cold and dull. The strength she had gained from feeding on my emotions would keep her in this state for weeks.

"You always have the most delicious memories," she said, licking her plump red lips.

Shaking and shivering, I wrapped my arms around myself. Coming down from the drug-like stupor was always hard, doubly so when you also had to pack up the memories and emotions you had worked so hard to keep locked away. I couldn't help but glare at the strigoi as she luxuriated in the feel of her latest meal.

"Now it's your turn," I said through chattering teeth. "Tell me."

Selma smiled languidly, blinking slowly as she focused on my face. "Go back to the beginning, Jack Dahlish. Do it quickly. You will find what you seek there."

I stared at her, disbelieving. The bitch had dragged me through one of the top three worst memories of my life, only to tell me to go back to the beginning?

"What the hell does that even mean?" I yelled out.

Her face didn't change, still too satisfied with the meal that would keep her going for weeks. "The beginning," she said simply, turning away to disappear between the tents and boxes on the far side of the homeless camp's shadow realm reflection.

"What beginning?" I asked quietly, staring after her in total confusion.

9

Crawling back into the normal world, I felt drained and used up. Having one's emotions sucked away to feed a supernatural creature is an experience that's hard to describe. It's like watching your childhood pet die in front of you, then having your parents and siblings drop dead moments later, all while every precious possession you've ever owned was burned to ashes.

The homeless people still huddling around the fire for warmth weren't casting angry glances at me now. Instead, they looked at me with fear and suspicion. I could hear them muttering to each other, about witches and fools that pay visits to them. It was rare for anyone to visit the shadow realm, and even rarer for that person to survive and come out again.

Time passed differently in the home of the strigoi. What had felt like hours to me was instead no more than a few minutes. Even with a slow, tired shamble I was back at my car only forty minutes after leaving it. I pressed the button to start the engine, and cranked the heat up to get warm as soon as possible.

Selma had said to go back to the beginning, but what beginning? The beginning of the kidnappings, assuming they were all connected? The place that Penny was abducted, as the beginning of the case I was brought in on? Or maybe the beginning of the day, the auto shop that I had spent an hour of the morning watching?

Yelling in frustration, I banged my hands on the steering wheel a few times. I had gone to Selma for answers, and instead it felt like I had more questions. A large part of me was tempted to go back to the Den and crash the Nox party out of pure spite. It would serve Richard right for sending me to see the strigoi on what felt like a fool's errand.

I dug into the center console, pulling out my phone from where I had left it while I ventured into the homeless camp. There were two missed calls and one voicemail, all from Ollie. After checking the clock to make sure it wasn't too late, I hit the button to call him back. I leaned back against the warming seats and listened to the speakerphone ringing.

"Jack?" the richly deep voice asked, shaking me out of a light doze I had slipped into without realizing it.

"Ollie. I saw you called. What's up?"

"You didn't listen to the voicemail, did you?" I could hear him fighting back laughter.

"I figured I would call and get it from the horse's mouth. Did you find something new for me?"

"Haven't had a chance to even look, I'm afraid. The rook and I spent most of the day directing traffic at accident sites. I swear the people in this city will never learn how to drive."

I felt another crushing weight of added disappointment. "What do you think about the theory that all the child abductions could be connected?" I'd mentioned the other kidnappings on one of my rambling voicemails, highlighting my conversation with the reporter.

"Karen Kilgraff," he said musingly. "Do you know how often that lady shows up at crime scenes before a reporter should even know that something is happening? As much as she can be a serious pain in the ass, I'd say that she has some really good sources. Wouldn't hurt to follow up on what she thinks she's found."

Sighing, I forced my eyes open so that I wouldn't drift off again. "I did check out one of the parks where a kid went missing. I can't be sure, but it feels like the same kind of Nox is involved. Probably the same person. There's an essence in both places that I've never felt before, and it's proving difficult to track down."

"I didn't think there was much you hadn't seen in the last ten years, Jack. I know you won't talk about it much with someone like me, but I think that if I was chasing after someone that didn't fit any of the molds I'm used to seeing I'd take extra caution. Are you being careful?"

Thinking about the recent visit to the strigoi and trying to keep it out of my voice, I nodded. "Yeah, careful. You know me, most careful guy in town."

"Uh huh. I do know you, which is why I worry." A voice called out in the background, too muffled for me to hear over the speakerphone. "Sandra said you should come over, talk it out while we grill a couple of steaks."

"BBQ in the cold? No thanks." I couldn't help but smile, knowing that Ollie would grill up steaks in sleet and snow the rare times we had that in San Antonio. "Tell her thank you for the offer, but I need to keep digging. Every hour that goes by makes me worry more about that little girl, and now possibly *those* little girls."

"I hear that," the veteran police offer said, decades of the same drive behind the words. "I'll go in a little early tomorrow, see what I can dig up on those other abductions for you."

85

"Thanks, Ollie. Stay warm by the grill. Tell Sandra we'll do dinner when this is wrapped up."

Ending the call, I slid the phone into the cup holder that was perfectly placed for me to see the screen with a quick glance while driving. I figured there was one thing I could do tonight to keep the case moving, even if it would mean a bit of waiting around. Throwing the car into gear, I drove out of the parking garage and headed north.

The KRSA studio was northeast of downtown, an old three-story office building that looked to have been around since the midcentury. The beige concrete walls left room for small windows, narrow but tall. There were half a dozen large satellite dishes on the roof, with a few more in a fenced-in section behind the building.

I had driven by hundreds of times in my life, but never actually pulled into the parking lot. It was almost full at half past nine, with the crowd of people working the ten o'clock newscast within the building. The heavy glass door opened onto a small lobby, with a black board displaying the names of businesses in the building. I was surprised to find that the news station only had half of the first and all of the third floor of the building, with the rest leased out to CPAs and lawyers.

Entering the elevator, I hit the button for the third floor. I felt confident I would find the studio there, along with the important people who would be putting their faces on the camera for tens of thousands to watch that evening. The elevator door opened on a boring reception area instead of the bustling action I had expected to see.

86

When I stepped up to the desk, the middle-aged woman seated there ignored me as she continued typing on her computer. Clearing my throat loudly finally made her look at me, her eyes and tight lips showing the disappointment that I was for interrupting her work. Belatedly, I remembered that I was wearing ratty and somewhat smelly old clothes for my trip through the homeless camp. No doubt she thought I was a degenerate who wandered in off the street with some crazy conspiracy theory to try and sell as a story.

"Can I help you, sir?" Her eyes told me that I needed more help than she could ever hope to provide, and I should leave immediately to find it elsewhere.

Pulling off the orange and yellow beanie, running a hand through my hair to try and straighten it, I gave her my best smile. "Hi. I'm Jack Dahlish, here to see Karen. She and I are working together on something."

"Mm hmm," she said, clearly not believing a word out of my mouth. "Sit."

Following her sharp-nailed finger, I saw a couple of old chairs with thin leather padding. The dragon lady picked up her phone and spoke quietly into it for several seconds before putting it down. She turned back to the computer screen and started typing away as if nothing had interrupted her.

I wondered if security guards would come through one of the two doors I could see, sent to escort me from the building with stern words not to return. It was frankly what I would have strongly considered doing if a client had shown up looking and smelling as I did right then. A brief thought of sneaking out to return the next morning in a more presentable manner flitted through my head.

A few minutes later the door closest to me opened. A young man stood there, a clipboard held against his chest and a headset with microphone over one ear. "You're Jack?" he asked me doubtfully. At my nod, he waved me to follow. "Miss Kilgraff said she'll see you after the newscast, and asked me to show you to the green room."

Smiling triumphantly at the receptionist, eliciting a har-rumph from her, I entered the sacred domains of the station. The green room turned out to be almost entirely beige. Beige walls, beige couch, beige chairs, beige tables. The only things not beige were one corn plant in the corner and a tray holding pastries on a small table. The young man left me there, with an admonition to stay put until someone came for me.

I looked over the food selection and picked up a slightly stale cream cheese Danish. Seeing the food had reminded me of the sparseness of my dinner, and started my stomach rumbling. Chewing the pastry, I walked over to where a small flat screen tv was hung on the wall playing the current content of KRSA. Some reality show nonsense that I could never focus on for more than a few minutes. Another tv above it, an old model twenty years out of date, showed the newsroom being prepped for the broadcast. Karen and a distinguished-looking older man sat side by side, reading over notes they had about the stories they would be covering.

A slight cough made me turn in surprise. A man with gray hair and beard sat on a chair that had been hidden behind the door when I entered the room. "You know they just keep the breakfast pastries out until new ones are brought in the morning?"

Swallowing the bite of pastry in my mouth, I shrugged. "I'm hungry enough that they could serve me last week's pastries and I'd be tempted." Stepping forward, I held out my hand. "Jack Dahlish," I said.

He eyed my hand for a few seconds from behind gold rimmed glasses before shaking it. "Professor Henry Morton. I'm here to comment on the latest financial policies the Fed have enacted."

"Ah, that sounds interesting." It really didn't, but it was always best to be polite.

"What story are you a part of?" The professor looked me over as he asked the question.

"Oh, I'm just here to meet Karen after the newscast." I said, letting his imagination run wild with the reasons for that meeting.

His eyes showed a range of emotion as he considered them all. I wondered if he had settled on the idea that I was a romantic interest, or perhaps some informant that fed her information from the streets. "Ah," he said, turning his gaze back to the television.

Smiling, I walked back to the food tray and shoved a couple of pastries into my pockets before grabbing another to eat. I was having too much fun shocking the stodgy old professor with my person-of-the-streets looks. The six day scruff on my face made it an easy persona to adopt.

I took a chair on the other side of the room, and watched the final preparations and newscast itself in silence. At some point, an intern or assistant poked her head into the room to call the professor out for his appearance. I even watched that short interview with interest, as the distinguished male anchor threw softball questions for the professor to answer and make himself look smart.

The entire time, I kept my eyes moving between the tv showing the broadcast and the older, smaller screen showing the studio as it really was. There was a lot of green screens behind everyone, which made me wonder why that wasn't called the green room instead of the beige room I was sitting in.

Karen was a joy to watch, the way she could seamlessly move from her normal manner to the smooth professional anchorwoman that spoke into the cameras. She never stumbled over a word, which was a skill I would have killed for when I could spend ten seconds just trying to think of the word I meant to say. She was all in shades of red once again, this time a soft-hued jacket over a silk blouse. When she stood up at the end of the broadcast, I could see that she was wearing a tight red skirt that showed off her fantastic legs.

Once the newscast was complete, the broadcast tv switched over to some late night talk show host giving his opening monologue. I ignored it and kept my eyes on the small tv. Karen and the male anchor traded barbs as they walked away from the news desk, words that I couldn't hear, but body language told me that they didn't particularly like each other. Which was amazing considering how much they had joked and laughed during the newscast. The studio slowly emptied, until I was watching a cleaner go over it to prepare for the morning show.

Fifteen minutes after the news ended, the young man leaned in and told me to follow him again. This time he wasn't wearing the bulky headset. I followed down a short hallway that passed by small dressing rooms where the on-camera personalities could prepare themselves to be presented to the viewers. He stopped at a door with KAREN KILGRAFF printed on the card stuck in a plastic holder. Knocking once, he opened the door and waved me through.

"Aren't you quite the eager beaver?" Karen asked, looking at her face in the mirror as she scrubbed off the heavy makeup worn for the cameras. Her eyes darted to look at me once, and then back again when she saw what I was wearing. "Please tell me this isn't what you normally wear when you go out to meet a lady?"

"No, I dressed up to see you." I pulled the orange and yellow beanie onto my head, making sure the tasseled flaps hung down over my ears. "Extra handsome. See?"

She laughed, a pleasing sound that sent shivers up my spine. "Shiny."

"Okay, I didn't think it was possible but you just got even more attractive." Pulling the hat off I walked over to lean against the counter that served as her makeup table. "I had to go talk to a contact under the interstate, and needed to fit in there."

"Now that I can understand. I usually have my sources meet me somewhere that they're the ones who stick out, though."

"Yeah. Selma isn't the kind of person you ask to come meet you." I could see interest building in her eyes, and decided to change the subject. "I stopped by hoping you had those reports on the other abductions. I checked out the park on the far west side, where Fiona Griffith was taken from. I have a strong feeling that you might be right, and at least that kidnapping is related to Penny's."

She said nothing for a while, rubbing at some stubborn caked makeup around her mouth. "I compiled the news reports, but you could have found those on your own with a little bit of Googling. Are you conjuring a reason to come and see me, Jack?"

"Karen, if I thought they'd let me in, I'd come up with reasons to see you every single day." She flashed a smile up at me before turning back to the mirror. "This time, I hoped we could talk about the separate instances. I'm sure you know a lot more about each abduction than I might find in the aired reports. And my cop friend won't have time to pull anything for me until tomorrow."

"Ah hah!" she cried in mock triumph. "KRSA beats the cops once again. Give me ten minutes to get pretty and you can take me out for a late dinner. How about that?"

"You're already the most beautiful woman in the building, Karen. But I'll happily wait ten minutes for you to realize it." I winked at her reflection, stepping outside to give her privacy. As I stood in the hallway, nodding at the occasional production assistant or gopher passing by, I tried to figure out why I was being so flirty. Yeah, I found Karen Kilgraff incredibly attractive. And yeah, redheads were my weakness when it came to women. But I had never been so openly flirtatious with a woman I barely knew.

I was still considering it when her door opened and she stepped into the hallway. She still wore the pink silk blouse, with the scarlet overcoat from earlier in the day draped over her shoulders. Her face was pale under the fluorescent lights, the red lipstick drawing attention to her soft lips. I presented an elbow, and she smiled as she wrapped her arm through it and we walked down the corridor together.

"Where should we go?" I asked. "This isn't my usual part of town, especially this late at night."

"There's a burger place a few exits west on 410. Absolutely divine, especially after a long night sitting under hot studio lights."

"Burgers it is. I like a woman who can enjoy the simple things."

"I enjoy all things, Jack. Some of them more than others." Her smile was seductive now, as I looked over and saw her staring at me. Before I could think of a response, we pushed into the little lobby. The dragon lady receptionist gave Karen a happy farewell, shooting a glare at me as we stepped into the elevator together. I restrained myself from spouting out a promise to have her back before curfew.

In the parking lot, I expected to separate but Karen kept hold of my arm. "You drive, Jack. That will give me more time to admire your handsome features." She reached up to stroke my stubbled cheek with a long red nail, causing me to blush.

I escorted her to my Honda, wishing I drove something newer and fancier, and held the door open so she could slide into the low seat. Walking around to the driver's side, I had to take a few deep breaths to center myself.

Once I started the car, she told me how to get to the burger place and then leaned on the center console with her chin on her hand. I could feel her eyes on me throughout the drive, unable to think of anything to say. It was the quietest two miles I've ever driven, and also the most pleasurable.

10

The burger place turned out to be a local institution that I'd heard of many times but never actually tried. We entered to find the place fairly deserted, the workers cleaning tables in preparation for closing at midnight. The older man behind the counter brightened visibly as we entered, and called out his greetings.

"Ms. Kilgraff, a pleasure as always. Will you have the usual?"

"Yes, Jimmy. Same for my friend." She was reaching into a pocket to pull out a credit card before I could speak. It was red, of course.

"You should let me pay," I said quietly.

She laughed, a throaty sound that sent chills down my spine. "Not this time, Jack. We're working, so I can expense it to the station."

Once we had our drinks, we found a table far from the counter where we could talk without being overheard. Karen's manner switched from seductive to all business instantly. "So, what did you find that convinced you the two child abductions are related?"

I had been dreading that question, hoping I could steer the conversation away from it. But like the pro she was, Karen had asked the one question I didn't want to answer right away before there was something else to distract her with. "That's a complicated answer. Let's just say that I work special cases, and I found something at both parks that convinced me they're my kind of job."

Karen smiled, her eyes crinkling at the corners. "Jack, do you really think I'm just going to take that as an answer?"

"I was hoping you might," I sighed. Did I really want to bring up the Nox and the hidden supernatural world to a reporter? Oddly enough, I could feel myself wanting to talk about it. I trusted this reporter more than I did most friends. I started with a question. "Have you ever heard of the Filii Nox?"

"Is that some kind of men's club?" She smirked at me with obvious amusement. "It sounds like a men's club."

Laughing, I shook my head. "I wish it were that simple. Okay, here's the basics. The universe was created by this massive wave of energy the ancients called Chaos. No one knows where it came from, if it was just a random phenomenon or directed by some unknown intelligence. For billions of years that energy formed the galaxies and all that's inside them. Yes, including the amoeba that eventually evolved into humans."

I paused here, knowing this was the point where people usually started to look like they suddenly remembered an appointment far away from me. Karen just looked interested.

"That energy also created the first beings that could be called gods. A handful of them, filled with the essence of Chaos that gave them incredible power. Over time, they tore off bits of that energy and created children of their own. Those created more children, a succession of gods both major and minor. Until finally the gods noticed humanity building the first civilizations and decided to try their own hand at creating similar beings.

95

"These creations were the first Filii Nox, the Children of Darkness. So-called because they were formed with pure Chaos energy, imbued with various abilities or curses. Your standard faerie tale stuff; trolls, vampires, pixies, werewolves. They're all real, they're all around you, and they're all very good at blending in with us normal humans."

I looked at Karen, surprised to see an expression of fascination instead of disgust or pity for the crazy man. "At the same time that the old gods were creating the Nox, a small number of powerful Relics were scattered across the Earth. Nine of those Relics give their wearers the ability to detect the Nox, to see and feel the Chaos essence they give off. I happen to have one of them, and that's why I know the two kidnappings are related."

Karen's lips were pursed as she listened, and she surprised me with the last question I would have expected. "What do they feel like? These essences?"

"Uh, it's kind of hard to describe to someone who can't experience it. I suppose it's kind of like getting into an elevator after someone with heavy perfume just left it. You can smell the scent that remains, you can move around the elevator and find where it's stronger or lighter, and sometimes it's strong enough to even taste. Nox essence is basically their perfume, except that it lingers for days or weeks. Sometimes months, if the creature is strong enough."

"Fascinating. Do you sense any of it in here?"

I grimaced, and shook my head. "It's not something I see or feel all the time. I have to open my senses to it, and that is an incredibly uncomfortable thing to do. I tend to just open myself a tiny crack most of the time, when I'm trying to detect the Nox."

"So I could be a Nox, and you wouldn't even know it?"

"Yeah, that is totally possible." I returned her smile, and shrugged. "Most of the Nox are just like you and me, decent and honorable beings. Some of my good friends are Nox, honestly, and I like them better than most human friends I've had. It's the few who go rogue and decide to harm humans or each other that I have to hunt down to capture or kill."

We were both silent as the older man brought over a tray with our food. Karen wrapped her lips around her straw and sipped soda, her eyes locked on mine as the food was delivered. "Thank you, Jimmy."

"Anytime, Ms. Kilgraff. You just holler if you folks need anything else."

I unwrapped a burger, suddenly ravenous. Taking a big bite, I chewed and watched as Karen delicately unwrapped her own burger and aligned the wrapper with the table edge. It was very much the sort of thing my sister would have done, that neat and precise movement of someone who like things to be in order.

"So, what do you think?" I asked as soon as I could swallow. "Call the looney bin, or check me into rehab?"

"No, I believe you, Jack. You would be surprised at the kinds of things I've seen in my years as a reporter. Hearing about these Nox helps a few things make more sense." She took a small bite. "Why haven't they ever been discovered, though?"

"Shape shifting, basically. All of the Nox have the ability to adapt human features, and it's rare for them to let that disguise slip. For several thousand years, humans did know about the Nox. They lived alongside us for centuries, but you know how humanity can be. The Nox were seen as abominations by some, who then preached against them and badgered others to hunt them down. After a thousand or so years of that, the Nox were few and struggling to survive. They adapted to better blend in and hide. Knowledge of them became myths and legends."

"Hmmm... I can see how that might happen. I'm sure if it had been the other way around, humans would have found some way to fit in with the Nox." She took another small bite of the burger, followed by a french fry. "And these Relics? What are they?"

"That one I really don't have an answer for. I know a handful of people who have one, but very few of us are willing to show their Relic. As you can imagine, it would be something a lot of unscrupulous people would want to steal."

She smiled mischievously and batted her eyelids. "So you won't show me yours?"

"The Nine are different. They're talismans, old coins hung on silver chains that can't be identified. They also become tied to the wearer over time, so that it's almost impossible to remove without killing us." My hand went to my chest, to touch it through my clothes. "Wearing one sets us apart, but also gives us purpose. Maybe I'll show it to you one day."

Karen stared at where my hand was touching the talisman for a while, and then looked away. Reaching into a pocket of her coat, she pulled out a USB stick and slid it across the table. "Well, back to business. That is a copy of every report on the child abductions. I threw in a few others that I don't think are connected, but happened within the time period. Eleven children total in the last four months."

"Those other three were taken from parks, too?"

"No, and that's why I feel they aren't connected. Two were taken from school playgrounds, and one from his home. Parents are main suspects in each of those cases, unlike the park kids."

"What can you tell me that I won't learn from watching the news segments?"

"First of all, the kids were all taken when the park was full of other children and parents. I spoke with a couple of the families after the abductions, and they all say that they visit the parks regularly. Often, they were at the same park just a day or two earlier when it was deserted or only one other parent and child there."

"That's odd. Why take a kid when the park is full of potential witnesses if you could just take them or another child when no one is around?"

"Right? That's what I found so odd. The other thing is that all of the girls had one thing in common." Her eyes glinted as she looked at me. "Care to guess what that might be, Jack?"

Munching on a french fry, I thought about Penny and the few things I knew about Fiona. The two girls had been opposites when it came to looks, one with Mexican heritage and the other a few generations away from an Irish ancestor. One dark, one light. One smaller than the other kids, and one already tall and gangly for her young age. "I can't think of anything similar."

"You're thinking of the superficial things, which all of us do. I checked the medical records where I could, and five of the eight have O-negative blood type. I'd say it's pretty astronomical to just happen to abduct that many kids with the same uncommon blood type."

"Huh." That made me pause and think. Aside from vampires, I couldn't think of a Nox that would care about blood. And even vampires wouldn't really care about the blood type, except for the specific flavor it might impart for them. So why would the blood group be important to whatever was taking these kids. "I'll have to check with Anna or Amalia in the morning, see if they can tell me about Penny's blood type."

"If that's what links them, Jack, then we have to be looking for someone in a medical profession. How else would they know what blood type each of these kids are?"

"Knowing you, Karen, you've already looked into that."

She smiled modestly, licking a few crumbs from a finger. "You bet I have. Unfortunately, the five I got the medical records for all see different pediatricians. Four of them went to doctors out at the Medical Center, but the fifth saw a doctor up in New Braunfels."

"That doesn't rule out a connection," I mused. "I remember a case Ollie was working on two years ago, some company that did all the paperwork for ninety percent of the hospitals and doctors in town. One of their vice presidents was selling medical information, got busted and tossed into a country club jail for a few years. Maybe this is a similar situation."

She frowned, her brows furrowing slightly to bring up a crease between her pencil thin red eyebrows. "I hadn't considered something like that. There might be someone I can call over at Methodist Hospital to ask about it." She pulled a small notebook from her inside coat pocket and made a quick note. "She gets in at nine, so I'll call her then and let you know what I find out."

"Hopefully I'll know Penny's blood type by then, too. I need to call Amalia and Anna to give them an update, anyway. I got so busy today that it slipped my mind." I sketched out the investigations of the day, leaving out the Nox at the auto shop.

"I remember that bank robbery! Ernie, one of the other reporters, said it was similar to a handful of others the station had covered. But then, a bank robbery is a bank robbery. Unless there's some kind of shoot out or flamboyant getaway, I suppose they're all the same."

It was my turn to write down a note, a reminder to look into those previous robberies. There was little chance it was even remotely related to the abductions I was working on, but meeting with Anna had given me a sympathy for Michael Castillo that made me want to look into his conviction. Perhaps there was something I could do to help him.

Karen was looking intrigued again after I put my notebook away. "Tell me, what does this essence feel like? The one you found in both parks?"

"Like old paper," I told her. "You know that feel when you're turning the pages in an old book made with really thin paper? Like it's going to fall apart under your fingertips? The smell was musty and very animalistic, but I can't place it. It felt so familiar somehow, like something I've smelled before but wasn't really paying attention to."

"Musty?" Her eyes lit up, and she pulled out her phone to start typing furiously. "You need to talk through your cases with me more often, Jack. What you just described reminds me of a story I did about six years ago, up in New Braunfels. You know that place just south of town, with the big sign on the interstate? The Snake Farm."

"Oh, yeah. I went in there a long time ago, with some high school friends. Tons of snakes, and there was this one pit full of rattlesnakes that creeped me the hell out."

"Exactly." She turned her phone, showing a video of a giant python shedding its outer layer. The snake was undulating, rubbing the old skin away. Dry, papery old skin.

"That's it!" I yelled out. "That's where I smelled the musty odor before, at that Snake Farm. I must have blocked it out to not think about all those rattlers."

"You owe me for helping out," she said with a wink, putting her phone away. "Do any of those Nox things have a snakey kind of appearance?"

"Ugh, so many of them." I leaned my head against the table, my brain running in overdrive. "Gorgons, basilisks, wyverns. So many serpentine Nox. But I've detected each of those in the past, and they were nothing like what I felt in the park. They don't give off the same essence this creature does."

"Okay, you are going to have to explain to me how something like a basilisk can blend in as a human sometime. For now, isn't there some kind of book or internet site you could look at to find out what the other people with your ability have seen through the years?"

I couldn't hold in a chuckle. "You are giving us way too much credit. The Nine tend to be very old fashioned and secretive, even with each other. I only know one other person who has a talisman, and only because he had to ask for my help when a creature he was tracking passed through San Antonio years ago."

"Jack, when this is all done, I am going to make you sit down with me and answer the hundreds of questions I have. I could write a book about all of this."

"Trust me, it would be a boring book. And no one would buy it."

"You'd be surprised, but I promise not to write it down as long as you share details."

"It's a date, as soon as we find these kids." I know the smile on my face had to look incredibly goofy to the teenager mopping the floor nearby, but I'm sure he could understand the fluttery feeling in my stomach that created it.

It was two minutes short of midnight when we left the restaurant, the old man calling out his goodbye wistfully. *Another man under the spell of Karen Kilgraff*, I thought. The drive back to the KRSA building was too quick, both of us occupied with our thoughts this time. I had several new leads to follow now, and I was impatient to get started.

It was enough of a distraction that I barely even registered movement before Karen was kissing me on the cheek and climbing out of the car.

I felt my face go deep red, a furious blush that was visible under the dome light with the door open. Karen called out a promise to call me in the morning before closing the door. Listening to the click of her heels as she crossed the nearly deserted lot to her red sports car, I had to force myself to focus on the case again. Being around the reporter was an intoxicating experience.

11

Somehow, I managed to get a few hours of sleep after tossing and turning on the mattress that lay on the floor of my small bedroom. I woke up feeling more exhausted than when I'd finally fallen asleep, with my mind still racing. There was a lot to be done, and as I was toweling off after a quick shower the strigoi's words started to echo in my head. "Go back to the beginning, Jack Dahlish." I still had to figure out what that meant.

I was craving my normal breakfast in La Villita, but couldn't justify taking the time to stop in. Instead, I went through a drive thru lane to get a cup of coffee with a bacon and egg biscuit. It would get me through the morning, at least. As soon as the clock read seven a.m., I figured it was late enough to call my clients and update them on my progress.

Anna answered the phone morosely, but seemed more eager when she heard my voice. "Have you found her?" were the first words out of her mouth.

"Not yet, but I'm working hard at it. I've got a few new bits of information to track down today that should get me closer." I could hear a disappointed sigh on the other end of the line, a feeling I could appreciate. "Anna, do you know what Penny's blood type is?"

"What? Why do you need to know that? Is she dead?" The woman was almost crying now, and I rushed to reassure her.

"No, nothing like that. It's just a theory that I'm working on. It's possible Penny's abduction might be related to some others that have happened recently."

I could hear the sound of a drawer opening and papers being pushed aside, and after a minute Anna spoke again. "She was O-negative, Mr. Dahlish. How are they connected? What happened with the other children?"

O-negative! It wasn't conclusive, but I felt confident that the other two kids Karen hadn't gotten records for would prove to be the same. "The other kids haven't been found, Anna, but that could mean that they're all alive somewhere. Keep up hope, and I promise I am putting everything into this case."

After reassuring her a few more times, I ended the call after telling her that I would update her again as soon as I could. Then I called Amalia and went through the same reassurances and promises. It was five days since the child had been taken, and I could hear the expectation of a safe return fading in their voices.

I drank the rest of my cooling coffee as I parked at my first stop, the location where the seventh child was taken. I figured the essence of the serpentine creature should be strongest here, only thirteen days removed from the kidnapping. It was a cold and cloudy morning, with kids still in school before the winter break. The park was deserted as I walked around the small playground.

Huddling in the warmth of my jacket, and missing the beanie from the night before, I opened my senses. The Nox essences were faint here, a place where few seemed to visit. That made the papery and musty essence easier to detect, stronger on my senses.

Gagging against the foul taste at the back of my throat, I followed it across the park.

I didn't realize my eyes were closed until I felt the brambles and branches tugging at my coat. Opening them, I saw that I had walked several paces into an overgrown greenbelt area that bordered the eastern edge of the park. Gingerly extracting myself from the grasping bushes, I stepped back and looked around. This area was far too overgrown for someone to have walked into the park from this direction, and yet the essence trail clearly led through it.

"Maybe they crawled?" I wondered aloud, crouching down to look at the leaves and detritus on the ground. It didn't look disturbed, but after two weeks the wind would have blown things around to hide any tracks. There was at most several inches of clearance below the thorny branches of the bramble bushes, nowhere near enough for someone to crawl through.

Walking back to my car, I had at least confirmed a link to this abduction. Next on my list was the site of the first abduction, more than three months before. I didn't expect to feel any trace after that much time, but I had to rule it out. That park was several miles away, so I called Ollie while I drove.

"Jack, I hope you appreciate what I do for you," he said when he answered.

"I always appreciate you, Ollie. Especially when you have good information for me."

"Well, I don't know how good it is. I'm reading through the reports on the abductions you talked about last night. Every one of them is still an open case, but there have been no leads at all. Each potential witness reports seeing nothing, parents and other suspects are clean and usually have alibis elsewhere in town. If I didn't know about those things you investigate, I would have to start believing in dimensional holes or whatever nonsense is out there these days."

"Dimensional holes are definitely out. The only one currently active is in the UK. Southern Kent, I believe."

There was silence on the line for several seconds. "You better be shitting me, Jack."

I held out as long as I could before breaking into laughter. "It's good to see that even a jaded old cop can be fooled sometimes. No such thing, as far as I'm aware."

"You have a warped sense of humor, Dahlish." I could hear amusement in his voice, despite the gravelly growl of his words.

"How about medical providers?" I asked, going through the theory that Karen and I had discussed only eight hours earlier.

"Same blood type, huh? That is a very specific connection. Too specific to be coincidence. Let me do some digging and see if we can find a common link between all of the kids' doctors. I'm going to have to take this one up to the detectives investigating the cases."

"I'm sure they can make better progress on something like that than I can. Just make sure they keep you in the loop."

"So I can keep *you* in the loop. You got it, Jack."

At the next park, in a very wealthy neighborhood, I found a lot of joggers running along the gravel path that circled the playground and ran through a small, forested area. No kids or parents again, which I was thankful for. Being yelled at by an indignant parent was something I hoped to not repeat.

This abduction had taken place after the kid was last seen bouncing around on one of those plastic horses on a giant metal spring. It was in the middle of the playground, in plain view of several benches that Karen's report had said were full of parents, and I couldn't figure out how anyone could take a child here without being seen. Especially at ten thirty in the morning on a sunny day.

Opening myself up again, I felt the cloying mustiness right away. Whatever had taken these kids had lingered in this park for longer than usual. Long enough to leave an impression that even two months later felt like they were standing right beside me. I closed off my senses immediately, leaning over and fighting the urge to puke.

"Hey, buddy. Go work off your hangover somewhere else."

One of the joggers was passing by, yelling at me when I felt my worst. I'm not proud of it, but it's entirely possible I flipped him the bird with both hands. Can't be confirmed.

This time I didn't try to track the path of the essence trail, afraid to feel it so strongly again. Whatever creature was here hadn't left that strong of an impression where Penny was taken, meaning that they spent a lot of time in this park. Perhaps they lived in the area. Or they had spent more time here because they were working themselves up to abducting a child.

Groaning, I knew that I would have to try and follow the trail to see where it led. My head was already pounding, the strain of opening myself more in two days that I normally did in two months. Wiping my mouth, trying to rid myself of the remnants of the essence, I steeled myself.

I made sure I was a dozen steps away from the previous spot before opening my senses again. Luckily, that precaution worked, and I saw the Nox essence passing several feet away so that the feel and taste were muted somewhat. It was heading away from the playground.

Keeping my eyes open and forcing myself to see the mundane and supernatural worlds at the same time, I followed beside the essence trail. It led along the jogging path, curving north as it entered the wooded area. That forced me to step closer to the path, the smell and taste growing stronger with each step. A few passing joggers gave me bewildered looks, no doubt wondering why I'd choose to walk through foot high dewy wet grass instead of on the dry gravel path.

After a quarter mile, the path split. To the left the trail continued on the circle of the park, while the right led north to a seven-foot-tall metal fence. Specifically, to the locked gate in the fence. Wrapping my hands around the bars, I tugged on the gate and found it sturdy and secure. There was a keypad with ten number keys, where the residents of the luxury condominiums the fence encircled could put in their code to go home. I could imagine the brochure for the condos, listing private access onto the park as a perk of buying a unit.

The Nox essence led through the gate, and I felt confident that whatever created it either lived in the condos or had at the time of the first abduction. Surely this was the beginning that Selma had told me to go back to, the first abduction. The St. Martin's Condominiums, according to the sign I could see across the manicured green lawn.

Walking back along the path, I put the name into Google and began going through the results. The price of a unit half the size of my house made me shake my head in horror, wondering why people would spend so much when they could buy a large house in the suburbs for the same price. Maybe it was the nine-hole golf course on the other side of the complex, or the shopping center with upscale stores a quarter mile away.

I couldn't find any kind of resident list, and when I put the address into one of the many websites I subscribed to that pulled up city and county records, it just spit out thousands of names. Rising professionals apparently bought and sold units here on a whim, moving on to somewhere even fancier as soon as they got that plum raise at work. Or when they lost their job and could no longer afford the obscene monthly dues.

Resigned to waiting for Ollie to get back with the results of the medical connection, I saved the names so I could do a cross-check later on. For the first time in two days, I felt like there was a serious lead to follow.

I drove past the main entrance to the condo complex a few times, taking a look at the imposing gates that prevented access. Climbing over the metal bars of the fence was an option, but in a neighborhood like this I knew there would be mechanical eyes on every inch of it. If I could find nothing by nightfall, then coming back would be my best option.

Karen called as I was dancing triumphantly to loud music, singing off pitch in celebration. I turned down the volume and answered in high spirits. "Hello, beautiful. You are not going to believe what I've found this morning."

"Jack," she said, and her tone sobered me immediately. "There's been another one."

12

With the greatest of luck, I didn't get pulled over as I sped across town to the old overgrown park in one of San Antonio's poorest neighborhoods. Three police vehicles blocked the entrance to the park, barricades already out to keep the spectators far back from where the crime scene techs were combing the rusty playground equipment.

I could see a couple in their late twenties talking with a detective not far away. The woman was sobbing, clutching at her husband or boyfriend as he yelled and screamed at the detective that they needed to find his little girl. Karen was leaning against a KRSA news van in the parking lot, two other local stations also represented.

"Jack, I can't believe this," she said as I walked over. She looked so vulnerable in that moment, and she hugged me tightly as she lay her red hair against my chest. "It's always been weeks between the abductions, but now they took another one after only five days."

I ran a hand over her soft hair, enjoying the feel of her body against mine. "When did it happen?"

"A little after eight thirty this morning. The family came here to walk their new puppy, an early Christmas gift for the little girl. Her name is Samantha Quiroz, four years old."

"This breaks the pattern," I said in confusion. "I've been thinking about the previous abductions, and they were always at midmorning on sunny days. The essence trail almost always comes from the east, which makes me think the kidnapper is hiding in the bright sunlight there before approaching the kids. Today is cloudy, and it's too dark."

"It's an empty park, too." Karen pulled away and retreated to lean against the side of the van again. "There was no one here but the Quiroz family."

Feeling cold without her warmth against me, I pushed my hands deep into the coat pockets and looked over the barren park. "Something here doesn't feel right. I need to get in there and see what I can find."

"The cops are going to have it locked down for hours." Karen had a wry twist to her mouth as she looked over the activity. "The police brass are so worried about the press making them look like they don't care about poor kids that they'll throw everything into this one. I wouldn't be surprised if they keep the park closed all day while they're banging on doors."

Looking over at the street, I saw more police cars arriving. Uniformed officers were getting out and forming a circle around another detective. From the few words I could hear, it sounded like he was giving a description of the girl so that they could start canvassing the surrounding homes and businesses.

Ollie stepped out of one of the last cars to arrive, seeing my wave and nodding. A young woman climbed out from the passenger side. I would have figured she should still be in high school if I hadn't seen her in uniform. She was barely five foot tall, if that, with black hair tied back in a short ponytail. The rookie, finally revealed after all I'd heard about her.

I stood near Karen for ten minutes, telling her about my morning. We watched the techs comb the park, and the huddled conference with the uniformed cops. When that broke up as they paired off to begin knocking on doors, Karen straightened and banged on the van a couple of times. She smiled over at me as the camera operator exited the rear doors.

"Time for me to get to work," she said, straightening her collar where a small microphone was clipped. I watched as she hurried across to the detective, the cameraman jogging behind her with a long cable that connected inside the van.

Unable to resist the temptation, I leaned around the open rear door and peeked inside at all the monitors and wiring inside the van. It was like a miniature production area, and I was sure the camera guy spent more hours in there editing segments than he did actually getting to film things.

The other two news crews were slower to notice the unoccupied detective, rushing over when Karen already had her large old-fashioned microphone up in front of the man's face. I grinned at my feisty reporter getting a leg up on the competition, confident that she would have a lead story for the day's broadcasts.

Ollie veered in my direction, shaking his head when he noticed my object of interest. "You and that reporter working together is going to be a real pain in my ass, isn't it?"

"Do I really need any help to be a pain?" I asked with a wink. The younger cop was bobbing along in Ollie's wake, and I leaned over to give her a wave. "Hi. Jack Dahlish."

"This is my rookie, who is far less of a pain than you are. Anne Bishop."

"Annie," I said, reaching out a hand in greeting.

She totally ignored me, cocking an eyebrow up at Ollie. "This is the P.I. you always talk about? This guy looks like the only thing he could catch is a cold."

"Ouch, I see you've been singing my praises." I looked the woman up and down, trying to figure out why someone so young would want to join the police force.

"Keep looking down at my tits, dickwad, and you'll be singing soprano." With that, she whipped around and marched away to wait by the sidewalk.

Ollie shrugged, his smile turning into a grin. "What can I say? She may be a dainty little thing, but she's got the attitude of a six foot bruiser."

"Uh huh. Better not call her dainty to her face, or you'll need Sandra to pick you up at the hospital."

"Better believe it," Ollie said with a chuckle, before his face turned serious. "What do you feel on this one? Same perp?"

It was my turn to shrug, as I looked back over at the dirt field that served as a playground. "I won't know until they clear the scene and I can get in there."

He looked at my face, his gaze boring into me. "Have you tried it from out here?"

With a sigh and an eye roll, I focused myself and reached up to place a hand over the talisman as I opened my senses to feel the essences around me. It was a heavily trafficked area, with half a dozen different types of Nox visiting often enough to leave strong traces. There was nothing that made me think of the serpent feel at the other abduction sites, and I shook my head as I closed myself off from the supernatural once more.

"Nothing from here. That really just says that whatever it is didn't come from this direction."

"Make a circle of the park, then. C'mon, Jack, we're talking about a missing kid here. Get it in gear."

"You're right. I'll circle around the block. Before you go, though, did you get anything on the medical connection?"

"I was still digging into it when we got the call to rush down here. Looked like the medical offices the first three kids went to all had a common medical records company. But it was one of the largest in the country, so that's not a shock."

"Ugh, and I'm guessing it would take all kinds of warrants to get any information out of those guys?"

"You bet. Lawyers out the wazoo, happy to get paid a few hundred bucks an hour to delay any kind of exploratory warrants."

"It was such a good possibility, too." I told him about the condo complex near the site of the first abduction, and my hope to cross reference a list of current and past residents with employees who had access to the kids' medical records.

"It's a shame we couldn't do that," Ollie said remorsefully. "That sounds like it could be promising. I'm sure the detectives will get started on the warrants, just in case we can't figure this out in the next week or two. That's about how long it would take to get anything from the medical company."

I watched Ollie walk away to where the rookie stood glaring daggers at me, and wondered why investigations always hit such difficult stumbling blocks when things looked so promising. I also wondered why Annie was so tough and gruff, but that was a mystery for another day.

Karen and the other reporters were still tossing questions into a flurry of "no comment" responses, so I started a quick walk around the block that was the run-down park. Opening myself to the darkness of the supernatural world for the fourth time in two hours was rough, the vertigo and nausea growing stronger by the minute.

After the first few steps, I was almost running in my rush to get it done. I'm sure there were speed walking records being broken as I circled the park as quickly as my legs could move. By the time I got back to the news vans I was puffing hard and even sweating in the cold air, but there had been no trace of the papery feel or musty odor. I was trying to convince myself to make a slower circuit when Karen spoke and startled me out of my focus.

"I saw you talking with Officer Williams. Did he give you anything?"

"No, we were talking about the medical connection." I turned to find her only a step away, our faces close together. "He said it could take weeks to get information from the medical records company, but so far three of the doctors did use the same one."

Karen was staring into my eyes, the small difference in our height mostly negated by her heels. "That's too bad. What's the next step, then?"

"Waiting here with you doesn't sound like a bad plan," I said, realizing I had leaned closer until there were only a few inches separating us.

She placed a hand on my chest, running it up and down a few times before gently pushing me back. "I wish I could, but we need to get back to the station. The cops here aren't going to give up any information until they fully process the scene. Even then, it'll be some sterile statement at headquarters. We got some shots of the park we can use for background to the story."

"Curses, foiled again," I said around a smile. "I'm going to hang out here for a little bit, try again to see if I can detect our abductor's essence before I give up. After that, I might go do some research."

"Call me later," Karen said, opening the passenger door of the van. Her camera guy was already behind the wheel and starting the engine. "Maybe we can get a late lunch, compare notes on what we find out."

Waving, I watched her drive away. I couldn't help but feel a little disappointed that she was leaving. Realizing that made me stop to wonder what was going on. I never felt this attached to someone so early. We weren't even dating, and a little flirtation didn't mean that there was any hope of a romantic relationship.

"Get it together, Jack." I pulled on the power of the talisman again and opened up to the supernatural essences all around. Forcing myself to take slow, measured steps I did another circuit of the park while fighting the rising bile in the back of my throat.

This time it took half an hour to circle the block, but again I found no traces of the snake-like feeling in the other parks. I was starting to wonder if the abductor had found some way to mask themselves from me when loud voices distracted my concentration.

Turning toward the playground, I saw the crime scene techs still plucking up almost invisible traces that could be evidence. A few were looking around, their heads swiveling to find the source of the voices. I followed the direction of their stares to where the mother and father of the missing child were waving their hands and calling out in loud voices. They were looking toward the far end of the park.

I turned in that direction to find a pair of uniformed officers escorting a little girl across the brown grass. The mother broke into a run, rushing across the park to drop to her knees and wrap the girl in a tight hug as the father hurried over. Little Samantha had been found.

Walking over to join the lone news van that had stuck around, with just a heavyset woman holding a camera pointed at the reunion, I was conflicted. Part of me was elated that the kid had been found, was safe, and got to have this little reunion with her parents. Another part of me was upset that I had wasted more than an hour trying to tie this disappearance into the string of abductions. It was time that I felt couldn't afford to be wasted.

I was digging my keys out of my coat pocket when I saw Ollie and his rookie trudging along the sidewalk back to their patrol car. Veering off, I called out and waved. Annie rolled her eyes, practically rolled her whole head, and changed direction to head back to their car along a path that wouldn't bring her near me.

"Can you believe it?" Ollie asked as he got closer. "They found the kid two blocks over, eating cookies with an old lady on porch steps."

"How did she get over there? Why didn't her parents see her leave?"

"It's hard to get much out of a four-year-old, but Samantha said she saw a ball rolling along the sidewalk and she wanted to play with it. The parents were doing something with the new puppy, so she just ran to get the ball. The wind was blowing it in the opposite direction of the park. By the time the girl caught up to it, she was kind of lost. The old lady was sitting in a rocking chair on her porch, called out to ask Samantha where her parents were." Ollie was shaking his head. "She said she was going to call the cops, but first she gave the little girl some cookies and milk and then they started talking. I think the old woman is a little starved for attention."

"I guess we should wish they all had such a happy ending," I said, watching the family surrounded by cops and detectives.

"You don't sound all that happy, Jack."

"It's just frustrating. I thought this would be the break I needed, a fresh abduction with a trail I could follow right to whatever is taking these little girls. I'm happy for *them*," I said, pointing across the park. "Just not happy for me."

"Welcome to my world," Ollie said, slapping a hand on my shoulder. "Investigations are ninety percent chasing down every little lead, and ten percent actual answers and action."

"Yeah, and I'm left with four more parks to visit, and only one clue that is pretty useless without something to cross reference with." I told him again about the condominiums near the park where the first abduction occurred. And about the long list of rotating residents.

Ollie wrote down the name of the place in his notebook, cramped writing fitting all the words on two thirds of a single line. "I'll run some checks on the address when I have time today. Maybe we'll get lucky, and there'll be a perp with a long rap sheet that makes them a good suspect for child kidnappings."

"Maybe," I said, not feeling much hope. Even if there was a likely candidate, the odds of them also being a Nox were larger than I could calculate. "See what you can do to make Annie hate me a little less, huh? I don't want your rookie always avoiding me any time we meet."

"Jack, I have been with this little lady for three days. You're the first person I've seen her even deign to notice. I'd say this *is* her liking you."

"Huh." I leaned around him to look at where Annie was sitting in the police car. Her dark mirrored shades covered her eyes, but she was turned in our direction. The scowl on her face didn't give me the impression that she was looking at someone she liked. "What does she do to the people she doesn't like? Kick them in the nuts and walk away?"

"Wouldn't surprise me one bit," Ollie laughed, walking away. I watched him climb into the patrol car, waving as they drove away from the park.

13

I spent a few hours hitting the last four parks, forcing myself through the increasing nausea and vertigo of detecting the essences in each. The snake-like feel and taste was present in all of them, to varying degrees. Nowhere was the strength of the essence as high as the first park, and the location of the sixth abduction was so faint I almost didn't pick it up at all. That seemed to indicate that the child taken there was perhaps a victim of opportunity instead of planning.

Sitting in my car, luxuriating in the seat warmers, I called Karen's number. Surprisingly, she picked up on the third ring. "Jack Dahlish, how did you know I was thinking about you?"

"I've been told that it's hard not to think about me. Like a vinegary old wine that was aged a little too long and lingers on the tongue for hours after a meal."

"Hmm, I was thinking it was more like a decadent piece of rich chocolate that leaves you wanting more after you've eaten it all." I could hear the smile in her voice.

"Want to meet for lunch? I just hit the last abduction site, and I could use some sustenance before I spend a few hours doing research in the library."

There was muffled talking, and I could tell she had put her hand over the phone to speak with someone else nearby. "One thirty, at Luigi's. It's a wonderful little hole-in-the-wall Italian place south of 410."

"You got it," I said. Checking the time and thinking about traffic, I knew I could be there several minutes early. "I'll get us a nice table."

The map on my phone directed me to the restaurant, in a tiny space at the end of an old block of stores. The lunch crowd was already clearing out, so I was able to get a cozy booth in a dark corner. It was far from the kitchen and the station where the two servers would stand between table visits, giving us a nice bit of privacy.

I was sipping the glass of water the waiter had delivered when Karen entered. It was as if the sun had chosen that moment to shine through the heavy clouds. When the door opened, a shaft of light entered the dim restaurant and highlighted the reporter in all of her vermillion glory. She spotted me and hurried over to kiss me on the cheek and slide into the booth on the other side of the table.

"I hope you weren't waiting long. My news director was ranting and raving about that poor girl being found so soon. I think he'd be happy to let his own kids stay missing for a couple of days if it meant a few extra ratings points."

"Sounds like a jerk, but I can't say much since I felt a little disappointed myself."

Karen reached out and placed her hand on top of mine. "I know, it was our best lead! Let's hope we aren't still searching for this monster before another kid is taken, though. That would be so horrible."

"Absolutely." The waiter interrupted, coming over with a basket of bread. He spent most of a minute spitting out the daily specials, and I couldn't help feeling slighted when he kept all of his attention on the redheaded reporter.

Pulling the menu from under my hands, Karen handed them over. "I'll have the scallop linguini, and the gentleman will have the mushroom and spinach ravioli." The waiter scribbled furiously and took the menus as he left the table.

"What makes you think I like ravioli?"

"Jack, do you know how many people I've had lunch and dinner with in all my years as a reporter? I almost always know what people are going to order before they do." Her eyes sparkled as she looked at me, flashing her white teeth in a bright smile. "Why, what were you thinking of ordering?"

Mushroom ravioli was my go-to dish in Italian restaurants, especially the first time I dined at one. Biting my tongue, I beat a hasty retreat. "Anyway, the parks didn't yield any more leads. The trails are there, but when I try to follow them in or out of the park they fade away within steps. There's too much traffic diffusing everything once you leave a protected space like a park."

Chuckling at my evasion, Karen cut a slice from the warm bread. She applied a thick layer of herb butter as she spoke. "My contact in the medical records office over at Methodist Hospital said that almost every practice in town uses the same big company to do their billing and maintain the patient records. I'm afraid we can't look to get any traction from that direction."

"That's why I'm heading to the library to do some research. Hopefully, I can find some kind of indicators that will give us a clearer idea of what kind of Nox we might be dealing with."

"Where is the library that holds such mysterious tomes where you can find data like that?"

"San Antonio Public Library," I told her with a shrug. "Sorry to ruin your fantasies, but there isn't a hidden library somewhere filled with esoteric volumes that contain the lore and knowledge of the Nox passed down through the centuries."

"Well, I can't say that I'm not a little disappointed. What kind of books would the SAPL have that could help you, though?"

"There are countless books I can look through, especially at the Central branch downtown. Roman and Greek Myths, Aesop's Fables, even Grimm's Fairy Tales. I know they all seem like silly little fictions that amused the people of their day, but a lot of those stories are built on truth. Tales passed down from father to son, or mother to daughter, warning of the kinds of creatures they should avoid."

"Like Hansel and Gretel, coming across a house made of candy in the forest? Snow White and her seven dwarves?" Karen was grinning now, trying to reconcile childish stories with what I had told her of the supernatural creatures that lurked in the world around her.

I baffled her by nodding. "Both of those are based on true events, passed in stories for more than a hundred years before the Grimm brothers put them down on paper. If you ever read Grimm's Fairy Tales, you'll notice the stories they tell are much darker than the saccharine versions in the movies or tv shows. The reality is even darker."

Our food arrived, and I could see her mulling over that information as we unwrapped our utensils and took the first bites of what proved to be a delicious meal. The ravioli contained porcini and portabella mushrooms finely diced, with fresh spinach and ricotta cheese. I could tell from the texture in my mouth that the pasta was handmade instead of store bought. It was rare these days to come across a chef willing to put in that much effort for a mid-range place like Luigi's. I added it to my mental list of restaurants I would swing by whenever I was in the area for a case.

"Even the old Greek myths I read in my long-ago high school days?" Karen asked after a long silence. "Medusa, with her hair made of snakes and a gaze that will turn anyone who looks at her into stone? What about the titans, like Prometheus who was banished for bringing fire to the mortals?"

"You're getting into complicated and deep waters, but yeah. A lot of that is real. There's a gorgon family living over on the east side that are lovely people. They throw the best block parties, and I get invited every year because I helped them out in my early days as an investigator."

She reached out playfully and poked a long red nail into my shoulder. "There's some muscle under there, but you don't feel like stone to me."

"That part of the myth is a little exaggerated. Their gaze only turns humans to stone if they really focus on doing so. No hair snakes, either, I'm afraid. That was just a writer trying to make his villain even more menacing."

"You don't know how comforting that is. I have enough snakes with whatever it is we're chasing, and I don't need more."

"After an hour or two in the library, I should have a better idea of the type of creature we're looking for. It has to be something pretty rare, since most of the old mythic creatures are well represented in the central and south Texas areas."

"Once you know the type, will that tell you how to find it?"

I chewed on the last bite of ravioli, holding out and waggling my hand in an uncertain gesture. "Maybe. Hopefully. It all depends on how much information I can glean from the old sources, and how much of it I can take as real and not invention of the authors."

"Well, make sure to let me know before you do something stupidly heroic like running headlong into a lair to try and rescue those little girls."

"You'll be my first call," I assured her with a smile.

Karen sipped the glass of red wine the waiter had brought with her meal, staring at me over the rim of the glass as our plates were collected and the ticket was left on the table. I grabbed it quickly. "My treat, since you got the burgers last night."

"Such a gentleman." She flipped her arm over to look at her expensive watch, and sighed. "I need to get going. The detective from the park this morning is in charge of all of the abduction cases, and he's sitting down for an interview that will air tonight."

"I'll make sure I tune in to watch you at work," I told her.

"Call me around seven," she said, sliding out of the booth. "We'll talk about what you find in the library."

"You bet, and you can tell me if the detective lets any juicy nuggets slip that don't make it on the air."

"I'll only share the good stuff with you, Jack." Karen kissed me on the cheek again, a lingering contact that sent a tingle through my body as she pulled away and I watched her swaying steps. Our waiter rushed over to hold the door open for her, staring after her like a lost puppy for half a minute once she was gone.

Waving my arm, I finally dragged his attention away long enough to come over to the table to get my credit card. I was wondering if this counted as a work lunch that could be expensed to my client, and then I remembered who I was working for and why. I'd give her a break on this one.

The drive to the library was quick, the traffic much lighter than I had expected on a Thursday afternoon. It was one of those great cosmic mysteries that Thursdays were always the busiest days on the road outside of rush hour. I had spent many hours in the car trying to figure out why, but the best I could come up with was that the stay-at-home parents saw the end of their freedom coming with the weekend and decided to enjoy a day out and about.

The Central branch of the library was far enough from my office that I parked in their garage instead of walking over. It was a perpetually crowded place, the multiple levels filled with college students, parents with young kids, and sometimes the homeless just looking for a warm place to spend a few hours. I had no problem with them being in the public library, unlike some who would make pointed remarks as they passed.

I found an empty chair near the history section, and draped my coat over the back to claim it before entering the stacks to find the books I wanted to look through. Grimm's Fairy Tales was up in the children's section, for reasons I could never understand, but I had a well-thumbed copy at home that I could check out in the evening. I pulled down half a dozen books on Greek and Roman mythology, along with another that described Mayan mythology. Snakes sounded like the kind of thing they might have had a few stories about.

My claimed seat was near a window that looked out on the hospital across the street. It was the perfect view, the kind that wouldn't distract me. It let me keep my nose buried in the books as I flipped through the pages. I was out of the direct sunlight, but near a vent that blew warm air on me from time to time.

The Mayan book proved a disappointment. After twenty minutes, the only serpent creature I had seen mention of was Quetzalcoatl, the deity they believed separated heaven from Earth and had a hand in the creation of mankind. If the Nox I was after had been anything close to an old god, the essence would have overwhelmed my senses and probably knocked me unconscious. I detected a god once, and it was an experience that I was not eager to repeat.

Roman mythology was really no more than Greek mythology with a change of names and locations. I spent half an hour reading through some of the entries, however, to make sure I didn't miss the rare mythical creature that was wholly a Latin possession. In the end, I opened the two Greek mythology books and compared a couple of the stories I had found to make sure the important details matched.

After that, I pulled down books on Norse and Egyptian mythology. Another hour was spent perusing through them, getting lost in tales that I had always loved as a kid. While most fathers will read stories like *If You Give A Mouse A Cookie* to their kids, mine would read to me of Thor and Odin. He was endlessly comparing the Norse myths with the Anglo-Saxon myths that were very similar. Much the same as the Greek and Roman mythologies.

In the end, I had two possibilities. The first was the Egyptian demoness Ammut, a creature that would eat the hearts of the dead found impure by Anubis. The problem was that the myths and legends all had the creature sitting at the god's side in the underworld, where Anubis sat in judgement of the recently dead. I couldn't find any reason for such a myth to be associated with a Nox roaming around on Earth. I certainly wasn't going to pop down to the realm called Hades, Hell, or Duat, among hundreds of others, and ask. Yes, it does exist. I've been there once. Don't ask.

The second was a Greek creature called a lamia. The myth stated that a woman named Lamia gave birth to children by Zeus. When his wife, the goddess Hera, found out about it, she forced the woman to kill her own children. The horrendous act turned Lamia into a terrifying creature that was torn by the agony of her act, goading her to hunt and eat other children. According to the myths, her upper half was a beautiful woman while the lower half was the long tail of a serpent.

Alarm bells were going off in my head as I read about Lamia in the book of Greek myths. I felt certain that this was the kind of creature behind the abductions of the little girls. There had to be a truth behind the myth, but I would need to find that to know how the Nox I was searching could be tracked.

Pulling out my notebook, I copied down all the data from the myth. The story about the woman killing her own children sounded like the kind of truth that could be distorted into a cautionary myth. Another tidbit that seemed promising was a throwaway line in one book about Hera taking away Lamia's ability to sleep, forcing her to live with the thoughts of her murdered children every hour of the day. Something that traumatic would no doubt cause sleepless nights and insomnia after being woken from nightmares.

I didn't like all of the stories mentioning that the lamia creature would eat children alive. That didn't bode well for the small girls taken from playgrounds around my city. In fact, it made me angry to think that a creature like that could be lurking in my town and I hadn't noticed or heard about it until at least eight innocent kids were stolen away.

Slamming the covers shut, I drew a few unapproving glares as I stomped through the stacks and slid the books back into the slots I had pulled them from. I tried to take some deep breaths to cool my sudden anger. Find the creature to focus the anger on, then let it out again.

It was nearly four by the time I left the library garage, and I turned my car south for my office. I could do some more internet research there, and run some searches on the sites I paid for memberships on. Based on the myths, men were ruled out as suspects. I had found nothing in all the page flipping to show that there was a male equivalent to the female lamia. To start with, I could search for women who had lost their children in the last few years. With an emphasis on those who had perhaps been suspected of causing the deaths.

It was a nasty little secret of the Nox world that not all the supernatural creatures came from long lineages dating back to the gods creating their first ancestor. Some, like the vampires, could turn regular humans into their kind. This was very rarely done, and then always by those who had gone power mad or saw it as a way to revenge themselves on humanity for long centuries of having to hide their true selves.

Others, though, were created when a momentary action was incredibly heinous or heroic. These overt actions drew the

131

attention of the chaos energy that still swirled throughout the universe, and in extremely rare cases the energy would fuse with the person and turn them into something different. It turned them into Filii Nox, the type almost always determined by the action that drew the chaos energy to the person.

14

Walking along the corridor toward my office, I was deep in thought. My eyes were on the ground in front of my feet, my hand digging out my keyring to unlock the office, before I recognized that there was a foreign feel to the air around me. The hairs on the back of my neck went up, and it felt as if the air was saturated with static electricity. The door of my small suite was open, and I could see a long shadow poking into the hallway from within.

I hesitated for longer than I like to admit, trying to decide if I should face whatever was inside or run away. Finally, I realized that running away wouldn't give me any answers, and I'd just torment myself with wondering who or what had sought me out. So I took steady steps forward, the sound echoing along the empty hallway.

Turning to enter the reception room, I saw a familiar figure sitting in one of the dusty chairs set up for visitors. He was facing the door, one leg crossed over the other at the knee and his hands resting lightly on the arms of the chair. The lamp beside him was on, casting the shadow I'd seen in the hallway.

"Mr. Dahlish, I was wondering how long I'd have to wait for you."

Closing the door behind me, I couldn't keep an accusatory tone out of my voice. "Most people have the decency to wait in the hallway or down in the lobby. They don't pick my lock to wait inside."

The man laughed dryly, standing to tower a few inches over me. He had looked far less imposing this morning at the park, with the crowd of reporters around him or while briefing the uniformed cops on what to look for as they knocked on doors. I waved him through into my office, glad to see that door was still secured.

"So what can I do for you, detective? Sorry, I never got your name."

"Cavanaugh," he said. "I sat down with Ms. Kilgraff a few hours ago to answer some questions about the spate of child abductions. She asked me some interesting questions, the sort of things that a reporter shouldn't have known to ask." He folded himself into the small chair where Amalia had sat two days earlier. "When I asked for her information source after the interview, she refused to say anything. But I saw you at the park this morning, Mr. Dahlish. It had to be you."

"Just because I'm in the same vicinity with someone doesn't mean I'm spilling everything I know to them." I hung my herringbone coat on the rack near my filing cabinets, and settled into my expensively comfortable chair.

"I should say the two of you are quite well acquainted, based on the hug I saw," he said with a faint smile. "Look, Mr. Dahlish, I think that you and I are working toward the same goal. We both want to find whoever is taking these girls and put a stop to it before another child goes missing. There is no reason that we can't pool our resources."

"Now this is a first," I said, my eyebrows raised in only partly feigned surprise. "The cops wanting to share information? Usually, one of you guys is forcing me to sit in a cramped little room pumping me for whatever I know when we're working parallel cases."

Cavanaugh brushed at a bit of lint on the knee of his beige trousers. "I'll admit that some of my colleagues believe that anyone outside of the force should not be involved in our cases. I don't share that opinion." He looked at me for several seconds before nodding, as if confirming something for himself. "For instance, I never would have thought to dig through medical records to learn that all of the children shared the same blood type. When Ms. Kilgraff asked me about that, I'm sure I looked a bit foolish."

"Karen is pretty good about asking the question you least expect," I said with a grin. "We only confirmed it for six of the kids, though. It's not a sure thing."

"It is now. I had my people check the remaining two and verified they also have O Negative blood. I don't know why that would matter, but something like that is too strange to be a coincidence."

It was my turn to stare at the detective for a while, as I thought about how much I should trust him with some of the information that I'd been working on. "Ollie told you guys about the medical records company, right? I'm betting that the person behind all of this is getting their information from a place like that."

"Medical records? This is the first I'm hearing of it." He pulled out a small notebook much like my own and scribbled as he spoke. "Explain your reasoning."

"The kids didn't go to the same doctors, or even the same clinics. They have pediatricians spread out all over town. The one link is that all of those medical offices must use the same company to maintain their records and billing. It's the only place that someone could find the blood type of all those kids, to know which ones to take."

"Hmmm." Cavanaugh continued writing. "Ollie is Officer Williams, yes? He might have talked with one of the junior detectives on my team. I'll have to check on that when I get back to the station, since that information should have been passed along. I'm sure Officer Williams mentioned that we would need a subpoena to get the information from the records company?"

"Yeah, and that it could take days or weeks. Maybe you can put your weight behind it, and speed things up a bit."

Cavanaugh smiled, but didn't comment on that. "What is your feeling on our suspect, Mr. Dahlish? Pervert, serial killer, child predator?"

I almost groaned, wishing he hadn't mentioned that last one. That was exactly what I was afraid we might be dealing with in a way, but I couldn't tell the detective about that. Karen may have accepted what I told her about the supernatural world, but Cavanaugh would lock me up in a mental hospital and conveniently forget all about me.

"I think we're looking for a woman who has been driven crazy by some things in her life," I said, trying to stick as close as I could to what I felt was the truth. "I think she sees these kids as replacements for children that she lost, or that she's driven to take them so that other parents can experience her pain."

Cavanaugh looked impressed. "That is almost exactly what the FBI profiler we consulted with told us. Do you have a degree in psychology?"

"Nope, but I have a decade's experience dealing with people from all parts of this city. That's better than any degree for helping you understand why people do things."

That earned another small smile from the detective. "Now you sound like one of our beat cops, the kind I go to when I want to know about the people of a certain area."

"How long have you had the profiler's report?" I asked.

"We consulted with him after the sixth abduction, though at that time we weren't sure how many of them could be connected."

"So you've known what to look for this last month, and didn't bother to share any of that information?" I could feel the anger rising again. If I had known about this profile two days earlier, I never would have wasted time investigating a revenge angle from the bank robbery or Emilio's old gang days. Possibly, I could have done the research sooner, finding the descriptions of the lamia and narrowing down my searches. It didn't help calm my frustrations when I remembered I didn't know about the other abductions until Karen tracked me down the day before.

"We don't share every piece of information, as you know. We have to keep some information internal to the investigation to prevent a muddying of the waters. If our perp knew that we had these details, then she might change her methods and make it harder to connect cases or track her down."

"Or, I could have known everything was connected from the start and not been spinning my wheels for the first day."

"I've been working on this case for almost two months, Mr. Dahlish. Do you think a single day would have helped you to solve it where we couldn't?"

Shaking my head in frustration, I rose and walked around my desk. "We'll never know, will we? There's every chance in the world I could have at least narrowed down my suspect pool. I think it's time for you to leave now Detective Cavanaugh."

He rose slowly, tucking his notebook back into his inner coat pocket. Pulling out a business card, he placed it on my desk and then brushed past. I watched him leave the reception area and locked the door behind him to make sure I wasn't disturbed again. Kicking myself for not asking if they had a small suspect pool of their own before asking him to leave, I settled in to run the searches I had thought of before finding the detective in my office.

Filling in the criteria on half a dozen sites, I kicked off searches that would comb their databases for women with children who were killed or taken within the last ten years. The best bet was that the tragic event was more recent, but I wanted to cover the bases. Once this search was complete, I also queued up a search to narrow it down to women between twenty-five and fifty with high income jobs or large injections of cash within the last ten years. That would help explain the access to the luxury condos of St. Martin's near the first park.

The faint light coming through the window told me that it was after six by the time I had the searches kicked off, and I figured those would take quite a while to run through the large databases involved. My library researches had burned through my lunch, and my stomach was beginning to growl and demand attention. Figuring that I could kill two birds with one stone, I swept up my coat and headed out the door for the cold walk to Lyon's Den.

Richard was behind the bar, as always, but this time the building was host to only half a dozen scattered patrons. Terrance was still sitting on his old familiar stool. I sometimes wondered how he found the time to run small-time cons on tourists when he was always found in the bar when I was there.

Grabbing a stool along the short edge of the L-shaped bar, I waved at Richard and mimed drinking from a glass. He nodded back, and wrapped up the conversation he was having with someone at the far end. I looked at the other patrons to make sure none of them were among the too large number of Nox that held grudges against me. Everyone was always happy when I put an end to a string of attacks or killings, but it was rare for them to think beyond the act to the families and friends that were left behind wondering who to blame. Mostly, that blame ended up on my shoulders, the easy target since I was already a bit of an outcast in the Nox world.

A pint glass was set down before me, filled with dark beer. I sniffed cautiously, pleased to find a slightly sweet smell among the hops and yeast. Taking an exploratory sip, I tasted hints of cinnamon and something that conjured thoughts of building gingerbread houses with my mom and sister when I was a kid.

"What do you think?"

"That's not bad at all," I said, taking a larger sip. "New addition?"

"Just got a couple of kegs in today. It's a holiday themed ale from a microbrewery up by the Pearl." Richard was smiling a bit smugly as he wiped at the spotless bar with his white rag.

"Getting ready for that Christmas rush a little early?" I couldn't help teasing him a bit. The Nox despised the human holiday of Christmas, most of them seeing the birth of Christ as the dividing line between when they were openly accepted and when they had to start hiding their true selves. As the single deity religion spread across the world, the old pagan religions faded into obscurity along with their beliefs that non-humans were not to be automatically feared and hated.

"If you ever dropped in, Jack, you'd know that it's one of my busiest weeks of the year. Lots of tourists love to bar hop and celebrate the twelve days of Christmas. Drunken frivolity at its best."

I grimaced, remembering why I had never stopped by the Den in the days around Christmas. It was also my busiest time of year, when resentment boiled over. Three or four Nox went rogue around then every year, forcing me to spend my holiday season chasing them down.

"Good party last night?" I asked, changing the subject.

"Every time. The Nox love having a place where they can let the proverbial hair down and just be themselves once in a while." Richard tucked the rag under the bar and bent so that we could talk quietly. "Sorry I had to kick you out like that. You know how it is."

"Hey, no need to apologize. I'd feel the same way in their position."

"Not all of them fear you, Jack. Just the ones who don't know you too well." He turned to look down the bar before grinning over at me. "And Terrance, of course." The Nox glanced over, as if he could tell his name had been mentioned. He frowned deeply in my direction before turning away and hunching over his nearly empty glass.

"Terrance isn't that bad," I said with a shrug. "I actually prefer him to all the people I have to track down. At least his crimes are minor, and don't really hurt people too much. I don't think many tourists are going to suffer because they lost twenty or thirty bucks."

"Don't let him hear that, or you'll encourage him." Richard leaned in a bit more. "How did it go with Selma?"

I groaned and rolled my eyes. "How does it ever go with a strigoi? I suffer through a top five worst memory in my life, and then she tosses off some vague fortune teller type of thing and acts like I'm a moron for not understanding." I tried to make my voice sound throaty and seductive, in imitation. "Go back to the beginning, Jack Dahlish."

I expected laughter, but instead Richard scrunched up his nose and pursed his lips in deep thought. "Now that is an interesting thing to say. Which beginning, though?"

"Exactly! I don't know if she meant go back to the first abduction or go back to the first person that brought me into the case." I took a deep gulp of the beer that got better the more I drank. "I did find something interesting at that first park, though." I told him about the strong Nox essences, and the trail leading into the luxury condominium complex.

"That sounds promising, but I don't think Selma would have sent you for something like that. I've never dealt with her myself, but those who have gone and told me of the experience afterward say that she always pointed them right in the direction they needed to go. Did she say anything else?"

"No, just that I should do it quickly."

"Beginning of the case," Richard was saying slowly. "Maybe it was a clue that the first person you dealt with was involved?"

Laughing, I shook my head. "I seriously doubt that. The grandmother of the eighth girl taken, Amalia, was the one who talked to me and convinced me to look into the disappearance. Back when I thought it was just a single kidnapping."

We were silent for a minute, and I drained the last of the delicious beer as we both forced our brains to try and make a connection that would clear up what the strigoi was trying to tell me. Richard finally shrugged and leaned back. "I bet it'll be something glaringly obvious when you figure it out."

"Yeah, just like any fortune teller. They'll mumble vague words that can mean anything so that when something does happen you automatically think that they truly have a gift."

"Don't knock it," Richard said sternly. "I've known some Gypsies back in the day that could really read your future. Some of the things they told me were not vague in the slightest, and every one of them happened."

Comments like that always got my curiosity pumping, and I spent ten minutes trying to get the bartender to talk about his past. He resisted, like always, good-naturedly but firmly. Richard had the supreme gift of mysteriousness that kept even an investigator like me at bay with ease. It was part of the charm of the Lyon's Den, and the reason so many Nox returned frequently.

Finally giving up, I told him to add the beer to my tab and left for the walk back to my office. The streets were packed with cars, people trying to get out of downtown and back to their homes out in the suburbs. There were more tourists walking the sidewalks than earlier in the week, people arriving in advance of the holiday less than two weeks away. Most of them would be admiring the beauty of the lights hung all along the Riverwalk for the Christmas season.

The searches had completed by the time I was back at my desk, spitting out eleven results. I felt a surge of hope when I saw the small number, until I started reading deeper into each one and had to rule them all out. Three were in jail for murdering their kids, four had seen their boyfriend or husband kill their kids and then committed suicide in the intervening years, three had moved out of state and not come back, and one was in a mental hospital up near Austin. There was an outside chance that she could be involved, but I couldn't see how her absence from the hospital wouldn't be noticed.

Swearing in desperation, I almost slammed the lid of my laptop closed. I turned my chair around so I could look at the lights of La Villita and the convention center that were visible through my reflection in the glass. For some reason, I had a strong feeling that I was missing something. It was a feeling that had been growing stronger since I left the Den, and no matter how I wracked my brain I couldn't figure out what it was.

The almost sleepless night must have been weighing on me heavier than I'd realized, along with all the strain I had put on my body opening myself to the supernatural world most of the morning, because I fell asleep at some point. It was the downside of buying a chair that was so comfortable to sit in, that it lulled you into relaxing when you shouldn't.

15

When my eyes finally opened, I could see the faint traces of dawn on the horizon. Groaning, and realizing that one of my hands had fallen asleep from being in an awkward position, I forced myself to lean forward. Pushing myself up with the hand that wasn't starting to feel like a thousand needles were piercing my skin, I stood and walked unsteadily to the hallway outside of my two-room office suite. There was a small bathroom at the far end from the elevators, and I used it to splash cold water on my face and wake myself up.

Staring at my face in the mirror afterward, I felt angry at myself. "It's not the time to be sleeping on the job, Dahlish. You have work to do and kids to find. You stupid idiot."

Suitably chastened, I pulled an old t-shirt from a drawer in my office to change out of the wrinkled mess that I had worn the previous day and then slept in. One of the many great things about wearing nothing but blue jeans was that they never wrinkled anywhere they shouldn't. Feeling a bit fresher with the clean shirt on, I grabbed my coat and rode the elevator down to the lobby.

It was bitterly cold in the early morning air, and I could see a bit of frost on the edges of the sidewalk. Hunching down in my coat and pulling up the collar, I walked quickly through the sparsely populated early morning. My stomach was growling fiercely, angry at me for feeding it nothing but a pint of beer since lunch the day before. I had a lot of thinking to do before I could decide my next steps, and there wasn't a better place to do it than my favorite café.

It had been only twenty minutes since the café opened when the bell tinkled over the door as I entered. The room was warm with the heat from the ovens, and there were already a few other early risers sprinkled around the room. I saw the familiar form of the waitress who usually served me the last four or five months, and I waved at my usual table. She nodded and grabbed a coffee cup and pot as I took my seat.

"You're an absolute angel," I told her, watching the fresh coffee steam as it filled the porcelain cup. "I'll have the pancakes and eggs, with bacon."

"Sure thing," she said faintly, walking away to pass my order on to the cooks.

I poured a packet of real sugar into the coffee, and then a splash of creamer from the little pods that were heaped up in a bowl on the table. Stirring, listening to the unique sound of the stainless-steel spoon hitting the sides of the cup, I looked out on the small walkway beyond the window. The square beyond a few other buildings was empty, the crowds of tourists still tightly tucked in their beds or enjoying hotel breakfasts.

Trying to figure out my next steps, I sipped the hot coffee and felt it warm my throat all the way down. I needed to call Karen, both to apologize for not checking in with her the night before and to find out if she'd uncovered anything new. We could discuss Detective Cavanaugh's visit, as well, which I'm sure would interest her. Beyond that, I wasn't sure what else there was for me to do but wait on new information from Ollie.

Reflecting on the conversation with Richard the night before, I thought back to Amalia, Anna, and Penny. That was two more people I needed to call and apologize to for not checking in the night before. I thought about the park where Penny had been taken, the slides that the little girl loved to go down over and over. I could imagine her joyful screams and calls of "Mom, watch this!" almost every time.

I replayed the conversation with Anna and Emilio, wondering if there had been any clues in something they said that I hadn't picked up on. My focus had been on the bank robbery and the absent father at the time, and I hadn't been thinking about it in terms of a string of abductions. It wouldn't be a bad idea to go back and ask them about the other kids. Maybe I could find some kind of tie that would unite the cases and give me a new direction.

That sent my mind back to Amalia, the grieving grandmother. It had been almost six full days now since her granddaughter was taken, and I knew that each of those days would have been increasingly harder. By now she would be growing more and more fearful that the little girl would never be found. Or worse, that she would be found dead, abandoned in some field or trash heap somewhere.

It was hard to believe that it had been only three days since she sat across from me at this very table. I couldn't even remember now which book I had been so absorbed in that I felt a strong dislike for whoever was interrupting my breakfast and reading. She had ignored my rudeness, however, and sat across from me to tell the story of the disappearance. It felt like that had happened long before, that the case had begun weeks ago instead of just days.

Begun. It was like a lightbulb going off in my head, that *Ah Hah!* moment that everyone talks about but never thinks they'll actually experience. This was where I had been pulled into the case, the place that I first learned of the child abductions. The little café where I ate breakfast most days was the beginning!

But why would Selma have told me to come back to this place? I was still overlooking something. I scanned the room, looking at the customers and trying to remember if any of them had been in the café three mornings earlier while I was talking with Amalia. None of them seemed familiar. In fact, the only person in the entire café that I could remember having seen before was the waitress. She handled all the tables on weekday mornings when the number of patrons was lighter.

I took a look at her, noticing her for perhaps the first time. Whenever I stopped in for my morning meals, I would always place my order and then never really look up again until I left the café. For someone who was paid to notice things and track down the leads that others missed, I was remarkably proficient at paying no attention to the people around me when I was in a familiar setting.

The woman looked around forty, perhaps younger but also possibly older. Her long black hair was a bit stringy, and her face was gray and wan. She looked like someone who never had time for themselves, carrying heavy emotional burdens that dragged them down at every step. The white shirt and long black skirt she wore under her blue apron were too large for her frame, making her look shapeless beneath the clothes. Thick woolen leggings covered her calves and disappeared under the skirt.

147

A plate was laid on the counter between the dining room and kitchen, and a loud bell rang twice. The waitress grabbed the plate, turning to walk it over to my table. Her eyes were on the ground at first, but when she raised them to look in my direction I couldn't hold back the gasp of surprise. These were the same dark eyes I had seen on the other side of the soccer field while investigating the park where Fiona Griffith was taken.

"Play it cool, Jack." Mumbling to myself wasn't exactly playing it cool, but I talk to myself. So sue me.

The woman's eyes slid across mine and back down, and she was silent as she placed the plate onto the table in front of me. The smell of pancakes, eggs, and bacon was almost enough to distract me, and I'm sure my stomach could be heard blocks away. I kept my eyes up, trying to see through the long dark tresses that fell in front of the waitress's face.

"Do you need anything else?" she asked, a trace of an accent in her words that I couldn't place. It almost sounded Middle Eastern, but I'm not the best at picking out accents.

"More coffee, please." I drained the three quarters full cup as soon as she turned away, afraid that my manufactured excuse to get her back to my table was too obvious. Watching her walk across the small room to where two pots of coffee were warming on burners, I saw that she had a sinuous quality to her movements. It was like the grace of a dancer coupled with the learned seduction of a streetwalker. Beneath the baggy and lumpy clothing, it didn't stand out unless one really looked for it.

Breathing deeply, I reached up to touch the talisman through my shirt. I had a feeling that what I was about to do was monumentally stupid, but I had to know for sure. Exerting my will, I opened myself to the supernatural world. It was the tiniest crack of exposure, since I wasn't sure what kind of pain might await. Sensory overload was always a danger when detecting the Nox essences, and I'd already suffered it once purely from the trail left behind by the creature I was searching for.

A wave of colors blossomed in the air around me, the streaks filling the small café in every possible direction. There were ochre and lavender streaks, but they were drowned out by the overwhelming blackness of the serpent creature I'd found in each of the parks where children were abducted. The cloying musty scent seeped into my nose and filled my mouth, making me cough and gag.

Underneath it all was a calming breeze that smelled of eucalyptus and the ocean. It was a seductive feeling, drawing me in and urging me to forget about everything else. *Come to me*, it called out, louder and louder as I felt myself giving in. *Join me and know true power!* I opened myself more to the world beyond that known by humans, falling deeper into the flow around me as I started to seek out the source of the voice.

My mind was pulled along on waves of the calming essence. It felt like diving into a deep pool of clear water, ripples of the essence flowing along my senses as it dragged me deeper and deeper. *Closer*, the voice called. *Come closer, and be one with us.* In that moment, there was nothing I wanted more. All earthly pleasures couldn't hold a candle to the temptation being offered.

A flash of red filled my vision. I wondered at that, wrapped in the lavender and eucalyptus that was drawing me ever deeper. Red flashed again, the color seeming to pulse through my brain. Instantly, I remembered a creamy pale face under red bangs. Red lips were moving, forming words. *Turn back*, they said enticingly. *It's not your time.* I paused, torn between the competing attractions.

Gasping for breath, I managed to pull myself away before I had given all of my being to the other side. My hand was clenched so tightly around the talisman that my fingers hurt from the strain as I forced them to open and pull away. "You stupid idiot," I berated myself through a shaking jaw.

There was a price to pay for the ability to sense the supernatural world, and because of my carelessness it almost drew me in fully. I didn't doubt that my corporeal body would have been left behind as a vegetable while my mind was soaring through the dark world seeking the source of the words that could never be found.

I looked over to see the waitress just now turning back to my table with the coffee pot. All of it had happened in mere seconds, when it felt as if I had spent hours lost in the lure of the voice. The taste of a snake's musk was still on the back of my tongue, as well. It all combined to make me look at the plate of food with a feeling that bordered on disgust.

In the silence, I heard the waitress approach and noticed the sounds for the first time. There was a faint whisper of noise that sounded like dry skin rubbing against itself. A *wssshhh* that I could hear with every step she took, under all the clatter of the other diners around me. It was the kind of noise that made me wonder what was under that oversized skirt and those thick leggings.

Swallowing, trying to get the foul taste from my mouth, I muttered a thank you as she poured coffee into the empty cup.

When she walked away, I reached out with a shaking hand to pick up the cup and take a sip. The bitter liquid burned away some of the musty taste, so I took another sip.

I was certain now that I had found the person behind the disappearances of the children. I had to be careful about how I approached it, though. Those kids could still be alive somewhere, and I didn't think this lamia was going to give up their location just because I asked nicely. If they were dead, I needed to find proof of that so that I could give the parents closure and the ability to fully grieve the loss.

Picking at my food, taking small bites and swallowing each with a grimace, I watched the waitress whenever she was in the dining room. I knew all of the waitresses wore nametags, but hers was hidden under the long strands of hair that fell over her chest. Paying more attention to my surroundings was something I was definitely going to have to work on in the future. Not that a first name would help me much. In a city with more than two million people living in the metro area, even a last name might not have narrowed the search far enough to be helpful.

The check for my meal was my last hope, since restaurants usually put the name of the server on the ticket to make sure any credit card tips went to the right person. When she dropped the paper on my table after twenty minutes, however, there was only a number listed. She was "Server #7", which was more useless to me than no name at all.

I considered trying to strike up a conversation with the woman, but that would have been so out of the ordinary for me that it definitely would have aroused suspicion. She was a Nox, after all, and even if she were a loner that never sought out the company of other supernatural creatures she would have heard of the man in town who carried one of the Nine. No doubt she had been watching me every time I was in the café for breakfast. Did it give her a secret thrill to stand so close to me those mornings, knowing that I had no idea who or what she was? Or did it make her afraid, and cause her to be more cautious around me?

Dropping some cash on the table, I slid my arms into my coat and buttoned it up tightly as I took a last opportunity to look at the woman. She was standing near the door to the kitchen, her eyes almost hidden behind the long bangs. I could feel her looking at me, though, and decided to give her no reason to think that I had discovered her secret. I walked out of the café, and half jogged along the path outside as if I had nothing more on my mind than getting back to the warmth of my office.

Once I was out of sight from the café windows, I circled around the row of buildings and examined the rear of the small restaurant. Beside a large dumpster were two older model cars and a beat-up pickup truck from the eighties. A sign over the one empty spot said it was for employee parking only. A glance around the area showed that there were at least two good places to observe this small parking area from. One I would have to be out in the open, and the other I could park my car and be somewhat warm.

Without a second thought, I hurried back to my office building lot to get my car. Along the way, I pulled my phone out of the coat pocket where it had been since the night before. The battery indicator was red, and I cursed myself for carelessness. Despite repeated mental notes to do so, I never remembered to buy a charger to keep in my car. I had one up in my office and another on my kitchen counter at home, and both were no help at that moment. The phone charger in my office was a cheap model I had picked up at one of those back-alley shops where the brand names were always one letter off from the real thing. It only plugged into the wall, and wouldn't work in my car. I felt fairly confident that the waitress would be working until after the lunch rush, but I couldn't risk running up to my office for a bit of charge in case she left early. I hadn't followed my usual morning routine, and that alone could cause her to spook. I had to hope she wasn't already making an escape, while I was getting into my car.

There were a handful of missed calls from the previous evening, from the very people I had wanted to call this morning. Karen had tried me three times and left a voicemail around midnight. Amalia called shortly after I'd fallen asleep in my chair, and Ollie had called the night before and again while I was making my discovery in the restaurant. If the ringer hadn't been set to vibrate, I would have been woken the night before during one of those calls.

I got into the car and drove out of the lot. It was still early enough that most of the downtown workers were on the way from their homes on the edges of the city, so I was able to park in a spot that had a good view of the back of the café but was also not obvious to anyone who stepped outside the door and looked around. The meter charged me eight bucks for a ticket that would get me to noon. Settling in as well as I could, I prepared for a long wait.

16

B y midmorning I had seen almost no movement from the café. Another car arrived at half past ten, a young man I assumed to be the second waiter for lunch and the afternoon shift. The sun was out, at least, and shining through the window of my car to warm me a tiny bit.

It was getting close to noon when I saw a familiar figure walking along the sidewalk in my side mirror. I watched him for a few seconds to be sure it was really him, and then rolled down the passenger window next to the sidewalk.

"Terrance!" I called out as he drew close to my car. I saw the Nox stop, hesitating as he considered whether to approach or bolt. There was no doubt that he'd recognized my voice from the one utterance. "I just need a favor, man. That's it."

He stepped closer, and bent down to look in the open window with a distrustful scowl. "Why should I do anything for you, Dahlish?"

"Look, Terrance, we both know that you don't like me. But we also both know that I've never hassled you in any way. I'm not asking you for some life altering thing." I held up my phone, now dead with a black screen. "Can you find some place to charge my phone for a bit? Maybe at the Den? Tell Richard I'll pay for your lunch and a couple of drinks."

He looked at me for a long while, and I thought for sure he was going to tell me no or just walk away. But then he yanked the phone from my outstretched hand and continued walking down the sidewalk.

"Thank you!" I called before rolling up the window again to keep the cold air out of the Honda. I couldn't help feeling that I might not see my phone again until I tracked Terrance down, but if you can't show a little trust to someone that hasn't given a reason not to be trusted, then you'll never be able to count on anyone.

Turning back to the view of the café, I saw a man in a filthy white apron leaning against the open door. He had a cigarette in his mouth, pulling deeply on it now and then before blowing out large clouds of smoke. This had to be the cook, based on the evidence of bacon grease and what looked like hot sauce spread liberally across the chest and stomach of the apron. I toyed with the idea of running over to ask him about the waitress, see if he knew anything about her that could help me out, but I knew he'd probably tell her afterward that someone had been hassling him for information.

I did get one helpful bit of data, when the cook unlocked and opened the creaky door of the old truck. He reached in to open the glove box and pull out another pack of cigarettes, throwing the crumpled empty onto the floorboards. Now I knew that the waitress drove one of the two cars that had been there since I checked earlier. Or she got a ride from someone who drove one of the cars.

Thinking about the glove box made me open and dig through mine. I kept a couple of granola bars stashed there for stakeouts or long trips when I couldn't stop for food. Ripping open the plastic wrapper, I took a large bite. It had been a long time since breakfast, and I hadn't eaten as much as I should have because of the snake musk stuck in the back of my throat. That had long since dissipated, and left me ravenous.

An hour later I hadn't seen anyone else enter or exit the rear door. I also hadn't seen Terrance with my phone, but I figured he might still be eating his lunch. Probably taking his time with it, too, and ordering the most expensive items Richard had on the single sheet menu. My tab at the bar was getting padded by a large margin, I was sure.

I'd just heard the bells of a nearby church toll a single time when the café's rear door opened, and my waitress walked out. She had a canvas bag over her shoulder and was no longer wearing the blue apron. She used a key in her hand to unlock the door of a peeling old car from the late nineties, sliding behind the wheel. I heard the engine fire up, sputtering and spitting.

"Shit," I said, looking down the sidewalk in the direction Terrance should come from after visiting Lyon's Den. I had to make a decision, and fast. Trail the waitress with no resort to calling Ollie for help if I found her lair? Or just get the license plate number and wait for my phone so I could call Ollie for an address it belonged to?

Her car reversed from the parking lot, and then turned to go down the street in the opposite direction. I pushed on the brake pedal and punched the starter button, setting my own engine into barely audible life. The quietness of the car compared to my previous vehicle was another reason I had finally purchased a newer model six years ago. Checking the mirror to be sure the street was clear, I pulled away from the curb and across all the lanes to turn into the small back street that ran behind the buildings where the café was located.

The waitress was turning left as I entered the street, her car mostly bare metal with small splashes of teal paint that had not flaked away yet. How could this woman be connected to the St. Martin Condos? Anyone with the money to live in that place would be the type to buy a new car every few years to keep up with the most fashionable models. Of course, they also wouldn't work a job as a waitress in a little café.

At the intersection, I was delayed by a long string of traffic that had just been released by a light turning green twenty feet away. By the time I was able to make the left turn, the old teal car was no longer in sight. I fed my car some gas, accelerating through a yellow light at the intersection. My luck was with me, and the next light was just turning green as I approached. A peeling teal car was near the front of the line, and I settled into the same lane half a dozen cars behind.

She turned left again at the next intersection. I was only two cars back now and keeping enough distance between us to not be noticed. Driving along Cesar Chavez Boulevard, I felt confident that we were going to get onto the interstate. A guess that proved correct when she turned north to take Interstate 37 past downtown.

Once on the interstate, the teal car continued traveling north in the middle lane. The waitress never went above the speed limit, which made it hard to stay behind her unnoticed. Someone going the exact speed limit is a rarity in any large city, and especially in Texas. Most cars were zooming past at five to ten miles over the limit, and we passed a few going five to ten miles under.

Not always in the far right lane, because people can't be bothered to think of others on the road.

I'm sure other drivers were thinking the same foul thoughts about me, honking as they swerved to speed past me. I got a few middle fingers held up in my direction, and knew I was going to draw more attention to myself if I kept trying to maintain her speed. Pressing the gas pedal, I sped up a bit and moved over to the left lane to pass the teal car. I turned my head away as I did so, in case she happened to look over. My car was one of the most common models on the road, and I could see two others of the same model and similar colors around us, so I knew it wouldn't draw her attention.

Once I was a few car lengths ahead, I pulled into the middle lane and slowed to go a few miles over the limit. Fast enough to justify being in the middle lane, but slow enough that I could still see the waitress's car in my rearview mirror. That worked for several miles until I was getting too far ahead, and needed to think of something different.

There was a maneuver I had seen on tv once as a teenager, and I'd always wanted to try it. I knew there was a perfect exit coming up, and decided now was the best time to attempt it. I moved into the right lane, and then again as an onramp became a fourth lane of the highway. The lane exited from the interstate, feeding me onto the access road where I could slow my car. After a quarter mile, I saw the teal car go by on the interstate as it continued travelling at a faster speed than I now was.

In half a mile, the access road had another entrance onto the interstate, which I took. The exit I had taken was for people who needed to turn onto the Parkway that passed over the interstate itself, and there was no light to potentially stop someone on the feeder road. As I sped up to a comfortable couple of miles an hour over the speed limit, the teal car was now far ahead and I had bought myself some time before I'd have to pass her again.

I didn't have to wait that long, though. A couple of exits farther on, the peeling old car moved into the right lane and then took an exit. Following behind, I took a right at the first light after seeing her do the same several cars ahead of me. This road was curving and following the dips and rises of the slightly hilly area for a mile before straightening out. There were shops and restaurants on either side of the wide road, but I could see houses beyond them.

Two miles from the interstate, the waitress turned into a subdivision. The sign showed the fanciful name of Glittering Meadows, and I tried to remember if I had ever been in any meadows that glittered. Trailing her on the residential streets was trickier, with the lower traffic flow. I had to give her a large lead of a couple of blocks, turning at each street after she did and often almost losing her a few times as she was turning again before I completed the last one.

When she pulled to the curb in front of a house, I was able to turn onto a street well behind her. I parked under a large oak tree, where I could just see the teal car through screening hedges that had been planted by whoever lived in the house on the corner lot between us. Her black hair was the first thing I saw, now pulled up and back into a doubled-up ponytail that still fell below her shoulders.

She looked worn and tired, and her movements were oddly stiff as she bent over to unlock and open the trunk of her car. I could hear the rusty hinges squealing even through my closed windows. I wondered if this was her home. It wasn't one of the nicest neighborhoods in town, but it also wasn't a run-down place where houses would be cheap. I didn't think I could afford even half of what a monthly mortgage payment would be here, though the woman's tips could have been substantial enough that she made more than I could scrape together on average.

The question was answered moments later when she straightened up and slammed the trunk closed. She was carrying a caddy filled with cleaning supplies, and had blue rubber gloves on her hands. A second job cleaning houses made sense, and would explain how she could have had access to the fancy condos. People like that almost always paid someone else to do the cleaning, and it was entirely possible that she had a few clients there who gave her the gate codes so she could get in and out while they were at work or elsewhere.

Now I was really kicking myself for not having my phone. I was dying to have Ollie check with the parents of the missing kids to see how many of them used a small cleaning service or paid a woman to do the job. Could this be how all of the disappearances tied together? The case that had brought me into this was a stumbling block, though. I hadn't seen any traces of a hired cleaner when I was at Anna's house. The home had been carefully tended, but it had the feel of being cleaned by someone who lived there and knew which spots needed frequent attention and which could be left for another time.

Half an hour passed as I sat in my car and watched for movement around the teal car. From the corner of my eye, I noticed the curtain of the house I was parked in front of twitching. I looked over to see a face in the window, an elderly woman. "Great, I just had to park in front of the window watcher." Every neighborhood had them, the people who didn't get out often and created excitement in their lives by observing everything that went on around them. These were the people who always knew which neighbors were leaving their trashcans out a minute longer than necessary or parking a centimeter too far away from the curb.

I could see a phone up near the woman's ear, and her lips were moving as she spoke to whoever was at the other end. Was she sharing the latest gossip about some weird dude hanging around her house, or calling the cops to report a suspicious person? My gut was leaning heavily toward the latter, so I resigned myself to finding a new place to park.

Starting my car, I waved at the woman as I started to drive away from her house. I had to laugh when the curtain dropped back into place as she hurriedly pulled back, probably unaccustomed to being seen peeping out of her window. The old woman's house faced away from the home my waitress was parked in front of, or I would have ventured to her door to ask for information on the raven-haired woman.

I had to go around several blocks of houses before I was back at the entrance to the street down which the waitress was parked. There were several driveways with no cars parked in them, so I pulled into one where I was able to see the teal car in my rearview mirror. The house I parked in front of had a jumble of junk stored on the small porch, which made me think the people who lived there were the kind to have a garage too full to park a car in. The driveway had black streaks from frequent parking and reversing, as well, so I felt safe in thinking they weren't home to protest me being parked there.

Three quarters of an hour passed in the driveway, as I slumped down enough to easily see the woman's car in my mirror. That also made it harder for drivers passing by on the quiet residential street to spot me. When the door of the house I was watching finally opened, I was grateful for something to relieve the boredom of sitting motionless. The waitress carried her caddy to the car, opening the trunk to store it away before getting behind the wheel.

She pulled away from the curb and drove forward, and for a moment I was afraid she might exit the neighborhood through a back entrance. But she pulled a tight U-turn several houses later, using a spot where another road intersected and gave her more room for the maneuver. The teal car drove toward me, rolled through the stop sign, and then turned to follow the same route we'd taken into the subdivision. I started my car and followed, keeping a larger gap than before.

Instead of leaving the neighborhood, however, she turned down another street and stopped in front of a different house. Putting my head on the steering wheel, I groaned at the thought of having to wait another hour or so as she cleaned an additional house. I watched the woman retrieve the cleaning caddy and enter a two-story home that was bigger than the last, and drove around for a while until I'd found another ideal spot to park and watch her car.

I thought about the small GPS trackers in my trunk, able to magnetically attach to the undercarriage of cars so I could track them remotely. Without my phone, though, they were useless.

They were also highly illegal to use unless you were tracking your own car because of paranoia that it might be stolen. If I found the place where she was keeping the children through such means, it would invalidate any case against her in the court system.

I didn't always have to deal with out of control Nox on my own, and quite a few have been turned over to Ollie for normal processing and jail time. Often, they would attack a human inmate and get tossed into solitary for the remainder of their lives, or tell a shrink what they were and wind up in a straitjacket for the trouble. Either was a satisfactory outcome for the less dangerous creatures. With a lamia, I felt it would be safe to have her behind bars. The legends all said that they eat only children, and she wouldn't have access to them in a prison. Her crimes would keep her locked away for the rest of her life.

17

P roving once again that being a private investigator is ninety percent boredom, I had to follow the waitress to a third house in the subdivision and wait outside again as she cleaned it. By the time she had finished and actually exited the neighborhood, it was after five and rush hour was in full swing.

That made tailing her both easier and harder. There were more cars on the roads for mine to get lost in, but I also got pushed back farther than I wanted several times and almost missed a light that the teal car had been through five seconds earlier. She drove southeast for most of a mile, before turning off onto a smaller road. I followed along curving roads with frequent turns as she went deeper into an area filled with older homes.

Just when I was afraid she might be cleaning yet more houses, the teal car turned onto a cracked and crumbling concrete driveway in front of a house with an overgrown yard. It was a small place, perhaps a thousand square feet. The neighborhood was forty or fifty years old, with wide lots that gave residents more privacy.

Her house had a sturdy fence blocking off the back yard. The wooden slats were fairly new and stained a rich brown color. Some kind of dark fabric was hung behind the fence, preventing anyone from looking into the back yard through the slats or knotholes in the wood. The fence was taller than normal, at least seven feet, which prevented anyone from being able to look over it without a ladder of some sort. On top were strips of small spikes, the kind sold to put around arches and signage to keep away roosting birds.

This was the place. I could feel it in my bones. The lamia had made her lair here, and built the fence to give herself all the privacy she needed. I drove by slowly, knowing that on a street like this I would stick out like a sore thumb if I tried to park and watch the house. But I was resolved to get a peek inside the house, to see if the kids were there.

It was already growing dark, the sun having set several minutes earlier on the increasingly cloudy December day. I found a small church around the corner from the street where the waitress lived, and parked my car in a part of the lot where it would be difficult for passersby to see it. Climbing out of the seat, I had to twist around and bend all of the kinks from my joints and muscles. Almost twelve hours spent sitting in a car can cause all kinds of hell on anyone's body. Ever since I'd hit thirty, mine seemed to find new ways to ache while doing things I had never thought twice about when I was twenty.

There was a black pullover sweater in my trunk, along with a heavy flashlight and pack of relatively fresh batteries. I folded my expensive coat neatly and set it aside, and then pulled on the darker pullover. A black knit cap and gloves lay underneath it, and I pulled them on, as well.

As prepared as I could be, I took the opportunity to relieve myself against a large tree while I waited for the twilight to deepen further so that I could walk unseen. By six thirty, it was dark enough in the poorly lit church lot that I could barely see my own hand when I held it out. The thick clouds hid the nearly full moon and wan starlight, helping me even more.

I found a small greenbelt that passed behind the houses on the waitress's street, a twenty foot wide stretch overgrown with mesquite and bramble bushes. I stepped quickly but quietly through it all, counting houses as I passed them. The lamia's house was the seventh on my right, and turned out to be easier to spot than I had thought it might. The tall fence pushed up against the small greenbelt, a solid presence unlike the sagging and cracked fences to either side.

Approaching the house from the rear showed me that the lamia had researched her choice of lair well before selecting it. The greenbelt floor was a bit of a valley at this point, with a steep slope of about four feet up to where her seven foot fence was built. Taking a risk, I clicked the button on the flashlight, holding my hand over the front to dim it as much as possible. In the faint light I could see strips of the bird deterrence spikes hung on the outer boards of the fence, about two feet below the top. She was serious about keeping people from seeing what was going on in that yard, a fact that gave me hope that the kids were still alive.

I checked the sides of the property, but found the neighbor's fences tightly abutted hers on either side. I could have easily scaled either of them, or just pushed past loose slats in one, but that would have put me in yards I didn't care about. Instead, I continued along the greenbelt to the end of the block, and then stuck my flashlight under my arm and shoved my hands into my jean pockets. Strolling along the sidewalk, I hoped to appear as nothing more than a late night walker to anyone that happened to drive by.

My luck held, and no one passed at all as I got closer to the lamia's house. Her metal and teal car was still in the driveway, with no lights on over her front door or around the garage. I was happy to see that. Her desire for privacy gave me the cover I needed to sprint off the sidewalk and crouch beside the old red bricks of the house. The only streetlight on this block was several houses away, the light not strong enough to penetrate to where I was hidden.

Creeping as quietly as possible, I made my way to the first window on the side of the house. I poked my head slowly around the edge to try and see through the glass, only to find that there was something covering the window to prevent anyone looking inside. Considering I hadn't seen any light from her windows at all, I felt a sinking feeling that all were covered in the same way. I had to be sure, though, so I continued along the side of the house until I hit the fence. Three windows, all of them covered with something on the inside.

There had been no noise from inside the house, and as far as I could tell the backyard was empty and silent. I tiptoed silently back to the front of the house, pausing to look up and down the street and make sure there weren't any pedestrians or oncoming cars that might spot me. The coast was clear, so I sprinted to the opposite side of the house to check the windows there. Only one three-paned window on that side, covered and silent.

Until I was turning to go back to the front of the house and heard a whimpering through the glass.

Freezing, I leaned against the cooling bricks and put my ear against the window. I closed my eyes and focused entirely on my hearing, waiting for a noise to confirm I hadn't imagined the whimpering. The seconds ticked by, and I spent at least a minute with my head against the glass. Long enough that the brick and glass warmed with my body heat.

My foot was starting to cramp from being in an awkward position, and I was shifting it when I heard the whimper again. It seemed to come from right against the other side of the window, and I could make out a quiet sobbing now. It was very obvious that at least one of the stolen children was alive, and only inches away from me!

I waited for another few minutes, hoping to hear more noises to let me know that other little girls were in the house. But there was nothing more than the crying of the single child. I had to get inside that house, even if it was only to save one small life.

Running in a crouch, I went around the wild untrimmed hedge to approach the roughly painted front door. I was hoping for cheap plywood panels, but as soon as I placed a hand on the door I could feel the sturdiness of it. This was a door built for security, to keep intruders out of the house. Hoping that luck was still running in my favor, I wrapped my hand around the cold brass knob and twisted. The knob turned a few centimeters and my heart started racing, but then it stopped and I knew the locks were engaged. Based on the other precautions around the house, I didn't doubt that the lamia had installed deadbolts not visible from outside, as well.

Hiding in the shadows, I considered my options. I could try to scale the fence to the yard behind the house, but I knew that the spikes would cause a few injuries in the process. And I fully expected that there were security measures on the other side, hidden until it was too late to avoid them.

My other option was trying to break a pane in one of the windows, open it, and get into the house. The problem there was that any half decent security system would have sensors to set off the alarm if the windows were opened while the alarm was on, and higher quality systems even put sensors on the glass to detect a breakage. All of that was aside from the fact that I would have no idea what was on the other side of the window as I entered the home.

This is about the time I started to really kick myself again for not having a phone charger in my car. If I could just call Ollie, he would come give me some backup. I don't think the sound of a child crying was anywhere near enough to get other cops involved, but Ollie wouldn't ask any questions about how I could be sure this was the place where our abductor lived.

There would be no shame in regrouping and approaching the house later with more resources, and I strongly considered retreating to my car and coming back a few hours later.

I was even taking the first steps to follow through with that plan, when a loud scream came from within the house. I could barely hear it through the thick door, which later proved to have a steel plate running through the core. It had been a high-pitched sound, exactly what you would expect to hear from a three- or four-year-old girl who was afraid.

That sound convinced me that I couldn't wait, and spurred me to do the stupidest thing I think I'd ever done up to that point of my life. I stood up, my jaw clenching with my anger, and pounded on the door five times with the side of my fist. How was I going to explain my appearance at her door? A woman who had seen me dozens of times over the last several months and knew my face well by now. I wish I had thought of something before I heard the sound of about a hundred locks being turned prior to the door cracking open.

The waitress stood behind the door, one eye visible as she stared out to see who dared knock. Recognition flared instantly, her eye going wide enough that I could see her irises were completely black. Pale lips pulled back in a snarl, showing me yellowed teeth with sharp incisors.

"You," she hissed out.

"Yeah, me. I know what you've been doing, lady, and I'm here to take those kids back to their parents." My jaw was set, muscles bulging behind my cheeks as I ground my teeth together. My hand was wrapped so tightly around the heavy flashlight that my fingers were starting to ache.

The woman laughed, a hissing sound that sent shivers down my back. She looked me up and down, and seemed to grow several inches as she straightened up from the slumped shoulders she normally adopted. "What are you going to do if I don't, talisman bearer?"

Which was an excellent question, now that I had just blown my one advantage of knowing about her without her knowing that I knew. I was standing on the step of a Nox that I had never encountered before, with no idea what her strengths or weaknesses might be. If I disappeared, no one would even know where I had gone after Terrance saw me many hours earlier.

So I did the only thing I could think of. I raised the heavy flashlight and whapped the butt end against her forehead through the crack in the door that had widened just enough when she laughed at me. Of course, I'd hoped she would crumple to the ground, not raise a hand to her head and say "Ow!".

I followed up with another smack of the flashlight, this time hitting her delicate looking fingers and smashing them against her skull. The lamia stepped back in shock and pain, and I was able to shoulder the door open and push through into the house. In the process, I shoved her back hard enough that she fell to the hard tiled floor.

Inside, the house was dark and filled with the musty odor I had picked up from the essence left behind in the parks. It seeped into the back of my throat until I was almost choking on the smell. At my feet, the lamia was sprawled out, and for the first time I saw what had been hidden beneath the black leggings she always wore.

Her legs looked like regular human appendages, but were covered in almost iridescent dark green scales. I swear I could see them expand and contract as she growled and got her feet set to rise. The shock of seeing those scaly legs was enough that I reacted slowly, swinging the flashlight too late. It whistled through the air over her head as she put a shoulder into my stomach and threw me back against a wall several feet away.

There was a loud crack as I hit the wall, and my first thought was a wild hope that it had been something in the wall and not something in my spine. Groaning in pain, I slid down to sit on the tiled floor. Cool porcelain tile was under my hands as they slapped down to try and take my weight before my butt hit the ground. If I hadn't known the woman was a Nox before, that display of strength from such a small body would have convinced me.

A thought which was driven from my head as a foot connected with my jaw, snapping my head around to bang against the drywall at my back. I could feel blood running down my cheek where her sharp scales had cut me. The kick also brought my thoughts back into focus, and I raised an arm in time to deflect the next one. Her foot impacted with my padded pullover, sending sharp pain through my arm but knocking her off balance.

Yelling in frustration and, I'll admit, a little bit of fear, I pushed myself off the ground and tried to tackle the lamia. I got my arms wrapped around her tiny waist, and my legs were pumping, but she didn't budge more than a few steps. A hand bunched up my coat around the middle of my back, and she yanked me around as she moved one foot back and twisted her body. I went flying through the air again, this time slamming into the top of a couch. Unfortunately, the couch was old and had a hard wooden backing with little padding.

Coughing, and wondering if this was what broken ribs felt like, I rolled off the creaking couch and onto the floor just in time to evade another kick that splintered the wooden frame. If kicking was good enough for her, then it was good enough for me. It sounded much better than struggling to my feet at that moment. So, I swung a leg through the air and felt my foot connect with something soft.

The lamia grunted and seemed to fold over as she retreated a few steps. My impulse purchase of steel toed sneakers a few years before had just paid off, making the extra cost more than worth it. It also gave me the time I needed to catch a breath and push myself up to my feet.

We faced each other, separated by at least ten feet. "Where the hell did you come from?" I asked through deep breaths. "And why are you taking kids?"

In response, the lamia jumped. Have you ever seen a wolf spider jump? It's a small arachnid that doesn't seem like it should be able to cover that much distance. This was just like that, and I felt the woman's legs wrap around my chest before I could even process the fact that she had covered the large gap with one spring. Her fists hammered at my head, hitting arms that I automatically raised to protect myself.

She may have only weighed a hundred pounds soaking wet, but that was a lot of weight to carry so high on my body. My legs wanted to give way, and it took all of my strength to push myself forward instead. I wasn't exactly running, but I got up enough momentum that when we hit the wall, I heard the lamia grunt. Taking the brief opportunity, I pushed at her chest and upper arm to try and get her to release her hold on me. It didn't work, and instead her legs seemed to flex even tighter.

My hand went down to grab at one of her legs without a second thought, and I flinched away as I touched her scaly skin. Gritting my teeth, I wrapped both hands around her knees and pushed with all of my strength to loosen her hold. I was able to draw in a deep breath again, but tiny fists started to pound against my bowed head which was now unprotected.

The strength in my legs gave out, and I twisted as I fell to land on top of the lamia. My shoulder was aligned just right to slam into her solar plexus as we landed, and I could feel the air expelled from her mouth. Her legs finally let go, and I rolled away to wheeze and groan.

"What the hell, lady?" It was all I could get out in my winded state, and I heard her hissing laughter again. I turned my head, jumping in shock when I saw that she was no longer where she had fallen. In the darkness of the house, I couldn't see her anywhere. I could barely see the wall I had cracked the drywall on and the couch that had somewhat broken my flight across the room.

The front door was open a foot or so, too heavy to swing all the way shut after I had pushed my way in. I really wanted to go through it and run as fast as my abused body would let me, until I reached the safety of my car. But I knew that was what the lamia wanted me to do. There was still at least one small girl in that house that needed to be rescued.

As if the thought had conjured it, I heard a little voice cry out at the rear of the house. I looked around for the flashlight I had dropped during the first rush from the lamia, and saw it laying against the door. It took all of my willpower to force myself onto my hands and knees so I could crawl the few steps to retrieve my only weapon, and then stand and turn toward the continuing noise.

I pressed the switch, and a bright cone of light filled the room. It looked like this was supposed to be a living room, but it was empty aside from the old couch that appeared to have been there longer than the fifty- or sixty year old house. There were two doors aside from the one that led outside. One went to the room on the left where I'd heard whimpering and crying earlier, and one led deeper into the home where I could now hear louder crying.

"Mommy!" a little voice called out. "I want mommy!"

My decision made, I rushed through the door leading deeper into the house. That put me in a long hallway, two doors to my right and none to my left. The far end opened into a room that looked like a kitchen, though I could see only a few cabinets with no doors. I could hear Ollie in my head, telling me to check the doors along the hallway to make sure a bad guy didn't lurk behind them. But the girl was still calling out straight ahead, and my heart drew me toward her.

The kitchen was gutted, one splintered door hanging from a single hinge over the spot where an oven should have been. There were cans on the counter, and I thought I caught a glimpse of pictures that looked like peaches before I turned the light in the other direction. Where a dining room should be was a row of cages made for large dogs, and in each of the cages I could see a little face blinking at the sudden light. A quick count gave me seven girls, but none looked like Penny. None of them looked like the lamia, either, which meant I should have gone the other direction.

"I'm here to help you," I whispered to them. "I'll come back, as soon as I find the mean lady, okay?" One tiny head nodded while another girl continued crying and calling out for her mommy. The others just looked at me as if they weren't sure to believe whether I was real.

I turned quickly to shine the light down the hallway, just catching the glimpse of a dark figure moving across the opening at the other end. "Ah, shit," I muttered. This was the part of a horror movie where I always yelled at the screen for the idiots not to go down the dark hallway where they had just seen something that was obviously the maniac killer.

So, I started walking down the dark hallway. This time, I opened the two doors as I passed them, flicking the light around an empty bedroom and bathroom quickly to make sure no one lurked within. Each time, I expected the lamia to come rushing down the hallway as soon as the light was turned. My muscles were starting to cramp up from being held so tensely. There had been no sight or sound of her by the time I was back in the living room, though.

The front door was still open the same couple of feet, and I shined my light around it. More than half a dozen locks reflected the light on the inside of the door, overkill for keeping people out of the house. That left only the unexplored doorway as the place that she could be hiding, and hopefully the place I'd find little Penny.

Stepping through it, I found myself in another bedroom. This one was larger than the one in the hallway, and wasn't empty. There was a pile against one corner. It looked to be dozens of blankets and quilts wadded up and propped against something to form a low roof over a small hole. *A snake den*, I thought.

Lying beside the makeshift den was another ratty sheet and stained old pillow. It looked to be right where I'd heard crying through the window earlier, but now I could see no sign of the child that had been there. I turned the light toward another door, leading to the back of the house. There was a larger bathroom, the master bath back when actual people lived there. Beyond, I could see double doors that must lead to the walk-in closet. Both were closed.

I nearly blinded myself when I entered the bathroom, shining the flashlight into the large mirror over a sink that was crusted with calcium and lime deposits from the hard water of our fair city. A hairbrush, toothbrush, and tube of cheap toothpaste were the only things on the counter around the sink. The bathtub was filled with water, steam still escaping into the cooling air of the house. The lamia must have been preparing it for herself when I arrived.

Swallowing the lump in my throat, I stepped closer to the closet doors. There was nowhere else for the lamia to be. My subconscious was telling me that she was going to leap out at me as soon as I opened that door. It was screaming at me *not* to open the door. To turn and run away, fast and far, and not stop until I was miles away from this horrid place.

My hand was shaking as I reached out for the doorknob, worn to a shiny finish from decades of use. I didn't reach out slowly as they do in movies, though. I pushed my hand forward quickly, releasing the door from the overhead ball-and-groove latch and pushing it backwards. At the same time, I twisted and pushed myself back against the toilet that was between the wall and vanity.

The only sound was my stuttering breathing, as I waited for what seemed an eternity before leaning forward and peeking into the closet. There were only five hangers inside, two empty while the others held a couple of white shirts and one long black skirt. I wouldn't want to wear jeans, either, if my legs were covered in scales.

Two little eyes were looking up at me from below the clothing, buried in a pale face that was frozen in fear. I recognized her instantly, from photos I'd seen online and on the wall of her mother's house. "Penny," I whispered as I kneeled down to be on her level. "My name is Jack. I'm here to help you. Where did the bad lady go?"

She didn't say a word, just looked at me. Finally, one tiny hand raised and pointed up toward the ceiling. *The attic!*, I thought as I turned my gaze and the flashlight to follow her finger. The light revealed stringy black hair hanging down, the lamia holding herself above me with supernatural strength.

Hissing, she let go of the walls and dropped, her mouth opening wider than it had any right to do. I crossed my arms above my head and ducked as her weight dropped on me. I felt her feet land to either side, and then her hands grabbed hold of my pullover and shoved me out of the room. I slid across the linoleum of the bathroom floor, flying into the bedroom. The friction of the carpet slowed me so that I only bumped my head against the wall. Shrieking in anger and triumph, the lamia was bounding across the space between us. A long, forked tongue was hanging from her wide-open mouth that looked capable of engulfing my head.

I tossed the flashlight at her, not even slowing the lamia as she dodged to the side and pulled herself forward using the side of the doorframe between us. She was one four-limbed leap away, and I had just thrown away my only weapon like a moron. I pushed frantically against the floor, trying to move out of her path as I saw her scaly legs bunch up in the light coming from the bathroom.

The lamia was in the air, a joyful look on her now inhuman face. I could see drops of moisture on her sharp incisors, and reflected that dangerous snakes carried venom glands above their jaws to feed through those fangs. If this lamia wasn't a dangerous creature, I didn't know what would be.

Time seemed to slow as my death approached, and I wondered if I would be eaten or die in agony from whatever poison she would inject into my body.

Two loud bangs filled the room, sounding as if they were right beside my ears. The lamia shrieked with pain and was thrown backward midleap. Two more bangs filled the room, and then two more a heartbeat later.

I saw the Nox jerk with each, and finally realized someone was firing a very loud gun. It was silent for a few moments, and I kept my eyes on the lamia until I was sure she wasn't going to jump at me again.

"Jesus Christ, Jack. What the hell *was* that thing?"

18

Ollie and I stood over the lamia, his large Heckler and Koch .45 caliber pistol still held by his side. Amazingly, even with six shots hitting center mass, she was still moving, and I could hear a quiet keening that reminded me of small, wounded animals. Her black eyes darted between us, and I could see fear in them.

Cold fingers gripped my hand, and I looked down to see Penny staring up at me. The girl had left the closet and must have accepted me as someone who would help her. Without a sound, she buried her face against my thigh and wrapped her other arm around my knee.

"Ollie, the other kids are in the back of the house, in the kitchen. She has them in dog cages. You have to get them out of there."

"Sure, Jack," he said, but didn't move. His face was filled with a weird mix of confusion and surprise, and I realized that this was only the second time he'd seen a Nox revealed in its true form. Knowing that supernatural creatures existed doesn't prepare you for the full reality of seeing underneath the human disguises.

I nudged him, and he finally looked away from the dying lamia. "The kids, Ollie. And it probably wouldn't be a bad idea to get more cops out here."

"Yeah." He sighed. "Yeah, I'll call the detectives and get some squad cars dispatched." He shook his head, finally flipping on the safety of the large pistol and sliding it into a holster at his waist.

"This is gonna be messy, Jack. How do we explain all of this?' He bent down and tried to take Penny's hand. "C'mon, sweetheart. Let's go help the other little girls."

"No!" Her cry was muffled with her face pressed into my leg. "Jack!"

"Ollie is a policeman," I told her, bending down. She let go of my leg and wrapped her little arms around my neck. "He'll keep you safe, and I'll be there in a minute. Okay, Penny?"

She nodded and reluctantly released me to grab onto Ollie's outstretched hand. He swept her up and settled her against his chest, and I could hear a faint sob as he carried her from the dark bedroom.

"My children," the lamia whispered, her voice quavering with pain. "You are taking my children."

"These aren't your children," I barked, turning to lean over her. "These little kids belong with their parents, who will love them and care for them."

I was shocked to see a tear fall down the side of her face, and she closed her eyes. "I love them more than their parents do. Almost as much as I loved my own children."

"I've read the old myths about your kind. You lost your kids, didn't you? And that turned you into the monster that you are now. Am I right?"

"Yes," she hissed out, her hands still pressing against the wounds in her chest and stomach. "I had nine children. Sweet and lovely children. Eight girls, and my little boy wasn't even a year old. But my husband wasn't happy." She snarled, and her eyes flashed when she opened them and locked her gaze on mine. "He said I was old, used up. He wanted someone younger, without the burden of so many children to care for. I would not let him go. I fought to keep him."

She coughed a few times, and I could see dark blood pulse from a bullet wound in her chest with each one. "His little whore wanted to be his wife. She thought getting rid of me and the children was the only way to make that happen, so she set fire to our house." Her hand reached out and grabbed tightly at my wrist, and I could feel the wet stickiness of blood. "I woke to the sound of my children screaming, talisman bearer. Can you imagine what that is like? I heard my babies dying in agony while I burned trying to get out of my bedroom and save them.

"When I woke, I was as you see me now. My legs had blistered and burned in the fire, but now they were hard with scales. The house was ashes around me, and I could only find bits of charred bone. That bitch killed my children, but she also killed herself that day. It just took a week for me to find her and put her through the same agony my sweet babies had to suffer." The lamia turned her head toward me, a wicked smile spreading across her face. "I made my husband watch as his whore burned, piece by piece. I made him listen to her screams the same way I had to listen to the screams of our children."

I pulled her hand from my wrist, placing it back on her chest where blood still flowed. "That was a horrible thing to have happen, and I can't imagine how painful it must have been. But it doesn't give you the right to steal other people's children. What were you planning to do with them?"

She coughed, and her mouth worked as if she didn't want to speak. "After I had my revenge, I left the village where I had lived. Something had given me another chance at life, I thought. I just had to keep my scales hidden from the world. But then, ten years later, I felt a growing hunger. An insatiable need that no amount of food could fill."

Now she turned her face away from me, groaning as she twisted her torso. "I saw a little girl in the street, walking with her mother. She smelled so sweet, so enticing. I had this urge to follow them, and when I did, I was drawn closer and closer. The mother noticed me, and she turned with a smile to ask if I needed something. Something inside of me broke, and when I came back to myself the mother was on the other side of the street with a bleeding head and the child was gone. So was my hunger, for a few days."

"You ate that kid," I said in horror. It was just as the myths as described.

"Yes, and eight more before the voracious emptiness inside of me dissipated. One for each of the babies I lost, talisman bearer. That was my curse, the need to kill children to fill the hole left in me by the loss of my own."

I could tell that she was fading away now. The bleeding had slowed, and in the wan light from the flashlight pointing at us from the floor of the bathroom I could see the blood was darker and thicker. "Then why did you take these little girls? You didn't eat them!"

"No, not yet. Ten years is almost up, and then I will have to eat children again to feed the curse that made me. But I wanted to have a family again, first. For just a little while. I wanted to be... a mother." The last words were so quiet I could barely hear them, having to lean down close to her face. With the last exhalation, her face went slack, and her hands slid from her chest to the floor.

I felt conflicting emotions as I leaned back on my heels. There was rage for a creature that would eat children just to keep herself alive. But there was also pity for a mother who had to experience such a devastating loss, and who had been turned into a Nox as a result.

Rising to my feet, I dragged my battered body into the barren living room. Ollie was beside the door, listening to the story I had heard. The eight small girls were behind him, holding hands and taking comfort in each other. When Penny saw me, she broke from the group and hurried over to grab my hand again.

"Cavanaugh is on the way," Ollie said quietly. "A couple of patrol cars should be here soon."

I nodded, and just looked down at the girl clutching my hand and staring up at me with trusting eyes. "We can't let them find her here, Ollie. They wouldn't know what to do with something like her."

"Take her away," he told me. "I'll say that I must have hit her when I fired, but she ran and I couldn't follow because of the kids."

Penny detached herself from me and rejoined the group of girls, as if she knew that I had to leave her again for a little while. Ollie led them outside, to wait in the front yard. He patted my shoulder as he passed by, and I knew he would give me as much time as possible before cops entered the home and swept it for any dangers.

I slid my arms beneath her legs and back, and lifted her from the floor. The lamia felt lighter now, as if in death she had become almost insubstantial. Carrying her through the house, I was

184

careful to avoid the corners. We passed down the hall, through the kitchen, and into the backyard through a door that had been chained and locked with another half dozen deadbolts. It was standing open, and I knew Ollie had anticipated the need to use it.

I found the yard empty, brown with dirt and small patches of dead grass. As I had expected, there were rows of barbed wire strung along the bottoms of the fence. If I had attempted to climb over from the other side, I would have cut myself badly trying to get through the looping tangles. Pushing through the coils gave me more than a few scrapes and tears in the denim of my jeans.

Where the strength came from, I doubt I'll ever know, but I kicked through a couple of the wide, sturdy planks until I had a hole large enough to stoop and pass into the greenbelt behind the house. A bit of the lamia's white shirt caught on the jagged splinters, leaving behind a small scrap of cloth. I considered it for a moment, and decided to leave it. Let the cops think that she had burst through the fence in her escape, even if it would cause questions about how someone could do such a thing.

Fifteen minutes later I was in the church parking lot. I lay the woman on the small strip of grass that I had parked beside, and reached into my pocket to press the button that opened the trunk. I pushed aside the jumper cables, first aid kit, and boxes of items I might need during a case. Once there was enough space, I lifted the lamia again and set her gently into the trunk.

I couldn't leave her there. If the cops brought in dogs to try and track her, they would head straight for my car. So I got behind the wheel and drove away. I don't even remember consciously thinking about it, but I ended up at the park where the first child had been taken. It was half past ten by now, and the park was deserted.

The walking and jogging path was still lit, but I didn't once think about the possibility of someone passing by as I carried the lamia into the wooded area. I turned off into a thick patch of trees and undergrowth, found a spot that wouldn't be easily seen from the path, and lay her down on the bed of fallen leaves. Her face looked almost peaceful, relaxed in death more than it could ever have been in life. I could only hope that her soul was experiencing a small bit of that peace, as well, wherever it had ended up.

I took a few steps back, thinking of how to dig a hole to bury her. At that moment, the body burst into flame. Blue fire engulfed the lamia's corpse, turning skin and bone into a fine ash within minutes. I could only stand and stare in amazement, feeling no heat at all from the flames that the woman had escaped so many years ago. Deep inside, I felt sure that she was being reunited with her children once again.

A quick glance around verified that I hadn't left behind anything that might make the cops show up at my door asking why I was near a pile of ashes found in a park. I walked back to my car with my hands in my pockets, and felt the first stirring of happiness. No matter how it had happened, eight little girls where going to be reunited with their families. It hadn't gone the way I'd expected or hoped, but I'd managed to save them with the timely help of a good friend.

I drove back to the lamia's house slowly, and had to park a block away. The cops already had a cordon set up at both ends of the street to keep people back, and news vans were parked and setting up nearby. Seeing Karen standing in front of the first van to have arrived, I smiled and walked slowly over.

"Jack!" she called out when she saw me, rushing over to take my face in her hands. She looked into my eyes and nodded once. "It *was* you that rescued the kids, wasn't it?"

"Yeah," I said with a shrug. "Ollie helped, though."

"What has been going on, Jack? I've been trying to call you since last night, and it keeps going straight to voicemail. Which is full, by the way, and won't take any more messages."

"It's a long story, Karen. A very long story, and not one for public consumption."

"Jack, you and I are never on the record," she said softly, wiping a bit of dirt from my chin with a tender finger.

I couldn't help but smile again. "Once this is all done, we can get breakfast and I'll tell you everything."

"It's a date, mister." She leaned in and kissed me softly on the lips. It lasted only a second, but I felt lighter and more energetic when it ended. Karen turned away and returned to her van, where the same camera guy as the day before was waiting with the heavy apparatus on his shoulder. He seemed to give me a small nod before I continued toward down the street.

Detective Cavanaugh was standing just in front of the saw-horses blocking the street, lit up by half a dozen bright lights as the reporters approached and waited for him to give them whatever details the police felt like giving out. He saw me passing by not far away, and raised his chin in acknowledgement. I could hear him start to speak as I passed through the cordon and approached the police cars in the middle of the block.

The house was brightly lit now, with work lights set up outside and within. There was a veritable army of crime scene techs passing in and out, carrying heavy cases and bags filled with evidence. Four ambulances were parked close to the house, and I could see a pair of the girls sitting inside each being checked over by EMT's.

Ollie was leaning against the hood of his personal car, right by the curb a few yards from the front door of the lamia's house. Two uniformed cops were standing close, one writing in a notepad as he listened and the other his rookie, Anne Bishop. For once, she wasn't glaring at me with visible disdain. Instead, she looked almost conflicted, as if she weren't sure how to feel upon seeing me.

As I approached, Ollie waved the two away. "I'll finish the statement later, Tom."

I leaned against the car next to him and crossed my arms as I watched the activity around the house. "How's everything going?"

"I won't lie, Jack. It's going to be a rough couple of days as I try to explain my story of what happened here. Which, by the way, is that you called me saying you had an anonymous tip that we should look into this woman. Safia al Hassan, according the DMV records on that junker in the driveway. When we got here, we heard the cries of kids inside and I made entry. She attacked us, I shot at her, but she ran away."

"The kids are safe, Ollie. That's all that matters." I looked over at the ambulances again, seeing Penny sitting next to Fiona. The girls were chattering away at each other, and I marveled at the resilience of young minds.

"Yeah, but the brass aren't going to see it that way. They're going to ask why I carried a personal firearm and checked a tip while off duty. And why I brought a private investigator along."

I shrugged and waved toward the row of ambulances. "There are eight families that are going to love you for saving their kids, Ollie. Your bosses can't fight against that. I'm sure the press is going to turn you into a hero, too."

His gaze turned toward me, and I could feel the tenseness in his body. "I'm not the hero, Jack. You are. Without you, we never would have found these kids. I heard what was going to happen to them, man. I'm going to have nightmares about that for months."

"You know it has to be you, Ollie. You need to take the credit for this, because there is no way in hell that anyone else here would believe the truth. If we even tried to tell it, we'd be locked up in a padded cell before sunrise."

"I know, Jack. It just pisses me off that I have to take credit for your work yet again. I get the credit, you get a minor assist, and everyone at the station keeps treating you like some scumbag P.I. that snoops on husbands and wives for a quick buck."

I laughed at the description, particularly apt since I had to take a handful such cases every month to keep the bills paid. "The people who matter know what went on here, and that's all I care about."

"Like the pretty reporter?" he asked playfully, twisting around to look in the direction of the bright lights around the lead detective.

"Karen does know some of it," I told him. "She seems to be able to accept the fact of supernatural beings hidden amongst humans."

"Very interesting. I'm glad I called her, then." Something hard tapped my fingers, and I looked down to see my phone. "Nearly every missed call on this thing was from her, so I figured I should let her know you were okay. I don't know how she did it, but she got me to tell her we'd found the kids, and fifteen minutes later her van was here. I swear the wheels were smoking from the speeds they had to reach to get here that fast."

I looked at the screen on my phone, showing dozens of missed calls and ten voicemails. "How did you get this?"

"Well, Bishop and I were having a very late lunch out on the west side of town when I got a call from that bartender. Rick or something? He told me that you'd been sitting in your car and asked a regular to charge your phone, and when the guy went back you were nowhere to be found. He sounded a little worried." I was going to have to show some serious gratitude to Terrance for that.

"As soon as we got back to the station late this afternoon, I caught a report coming in over the radio. Some old lady not far from here calling in that, and I quote, 'a creepy homeless man in a car that he must have stolen was casing her house and making menacing gestures at her'. Once I heard dark gray Honda, I knew it had to be you." He chuckled.

"Thanks," I muttered. "So glad I could be amusing for you. All I did was wave at the lady as I left, so she wouldn't be afraid. I was tracking the lamia... er, Safia al Hassan, from my café to find out where she was keeping the kids."

"Yeah, and you're going to have to explain that sudden leap from 'who's doing this?' to 'it's her!' for me tomorrow. Anyway, that told me your approximate location and let me check traffic cams. There's a red light camera where you turned onto the street near here, and I didn't see your car again after that. Once my shift was over, I drove out here and started looking.

"I found your car parked at that church, and knew you had to be nearby. This was the third street I drove down, looking for any sign of you. Then I see this house, totally dark when every other house on the block has at least one light burning, and that drew my attention. I was a few houses away on the other side of the street when I saw a light flash through the open door. That had to be either you or a burglar, and I couldn't ignore either one, so I rushed over and entered quietly. And then, well, you know what happened."

I placed a hand on his shoulder and squeezed. "I'm very grateful that you showed up when you did, Ollie. Two seconds later, and you would have been sitting out here watching them wheel my body away."

"Aw, I don't know if it would have been as bad as that."

"You weren't the one who got thrown across the room by a tiny little woman," I said, rubbing at my back, which was growing sore now that the adrenaline was fading from my system.

"That's what that dent in the wall was? Okay, maybe it would have been pretty bad."

We sat in companionable silence after that, watching the crime scene people work the scene. Cavanaugh walked by and nodded at us before disappearing into the house. The way the guy was acting, I felt like he knew something more had gone on than

Ollie was telling, but that he also wasn't going to push too hard to find out what.

"Jack!" a tiny voice cried out, and I felt a small body barrel into my leg. I looked down to see Penny hugging me, and looked at Ollie with a raised eyebrow.

"You've got a fan," he said with a grin. "She's been asking about you nonstop for the last hour."

I lifted the girl up to support her on my hip, and she hugged me tightly around the neck. "Tank you, Jack," she said, the adorable words melting my heart. The she pulled back to look me in the eye and frowned. "Where's momma?"

Suddenly I remembered my client and her daughter, and my lack of contact with them for the last couple of days. "You'll see your mommy soon," Ollie told the girl. "Uniforms were dispatched to pick up the parents and take them to the station downtown. Family services will meet us all there so they can arrange counseling for the kids."

Bishop approached, and she smirked when she saw me holding Penny. "They're ready to take the girls downtown, Sarge."

Ollie grunted as he pushed away from the car, and held his arms out. "Come with me, Penny. We're going to go see all of your mommies."

She looked at me as if asking if she should go, and I nodded. Her small arms hugged me again, and then she twisted around and raised her arms so Ollie could pull her away. He walked away to where the other kids were climbing into several cars, and I felt real joy to see them laughing and playing with each other.

"He won't tell me what really happened in there." I turned to see the rookie staring at me with her head tilted to the side. "But

I know he was trying to find you all afternoon, so there's no way you just happened to call him with a tip. Especially since he had your phone." She turned away and took a few steps before looking over her shoulder, loose strands of black hair sticking out from under the police ball cap. "You might not be so bad after all, Dahlish."

19

I was in my office early the next morning, watching the sun rise over the convention center. I'd like to say that I'd gone home and slept the sleep of the just and was refreshed for a new day, but I was bone tired and had been up all night. I stayed at the lamia's house until almost two in the morning, watching the cops and crime scene techs work. Mostly because I was afraid they would find something that made them freak out. My luck held, though, and aside from some comments about the weirdness of someone keeping kids locked in dog cages there was no clamor over anything they found.

By that time, the news vans were gone, and the reporters were back at the stations working on the segments that would air all day today on every local station. Probably on a few national channels, as well. Finding eight abducted kids alive was the kind of feel-good story that newscasts loved to air between rundowns of the latest carjacking or murder outside a bar or nightclub.

I had been tempted to call Amalia, to explain my long silence, but I knew that she and Anna would still be reuniting with Penny, surrounded by other parents joyfully greeting children who had been lost for too long. It felt wrong to interrupt something like that just to assuage my own guilt.

So, instead I had come back to my office. I tried to write up a report of the encounter with the lamia, something that would be stored in my very secure file cabinet in case I ever needed to refer back to it. I'd managed to get through half of the report by the time I noticed the sky growing brighter behind me. It was rare for me to be in this early, so I turned to enjoy the view of a new day dawning over San Antonio. A safer day.

The door opened behind me, and I swiveled around to see Amalia standing just inside my office. She was beaming, with tears of joy in her eyes. I rose and started to apologize for being out of touch, but she just rushed over and wrapped me in a tight hug that made me think of her granddaughter.

"Thank you so much, Mr. Dahlish. Our Penny is back, and I know it's all because of you." She released me and stepped back to look up into my eyes.

"I am so sorry for not keeping you updated," I said. "My phone died, and I had just discovered who the abductor was, and..."

"Mr. Dahlish, you don't need to apologize. You saved eight precious lives, and I would take a month of worrying and fretting about not hearing from you in return for that." She squeezed my arms, and then patted them. "I think our little Penny is in love with you. All night she kept asking where Jack was. She drew something, and said it was for you."

Amalia opened her purse and dug around a bit, pulling out a folded sheet of paper and handing it to me. I gingerly opened it and saw a child's rendering of a man surrounded by eight stick figures with long hair. They were standing on green strokes that I knew was grass, a big yellow sun in the upper left corner. In the background was a curving green shape that looked like a letter S. Looking closer, though, I could see two black dots that might be eyes and a smudge that could be a pink tongue.

For a moment, I wondered again how the lamia had managed to get the children out of the parks without being seen. Had she been able to shift into a full serpent form? If so, how would that let her abduct the little girls? I knew there would be sleepless nights during which I wondered about those questions and more, but my only source of answers wasn't around to be asked any longer.

"Is she doing okay?" I asked. "Did she have nightmares or anything?"

"No, gracias a Dios. She slept like a log on the drive to Anna's house, and was still sleeping when I left them. The police have a psychiatrist who is going to work with all of the girls. He wants to do individual sessions with each, but also sometimes with them all together. The only time I saw any of them cry was when they realized they would be splitting up."

I could imagine how close the girls must have become, all trapped in tiny cages next to each other while the lamia was out of the house. They must have latched on to each other, unable to come to terms with the strangeness of their surroundings and the woman who took them.

Amalia was staring at me, her eyes darting between each of mine. "Anna also got a call from Michael this morning. He was overjoyed to learn his daughter is safe, and told her that he's meeting with a new lawyer today. A lawyer that seems certain they can do something to get him out of jail soon."

She smiled, seemed to find what she was looking for in my eyes, and nodded in gratitude. I could feel the redness in my cheeks, embarrassed at being found out. I'd called in a few favors with an attorney I'd done some work for in the past. With what

I'd learned about the auto shop owner, he felt confident he could put together a deal to get Michael released in exchange for a little cooperative testimony that might tie together a string of seemingly unrelated robberies.

"Tell Penny thank you for the drawing. I'll hang it on my wall and remember her every time I look at it."

"What you will do is come and visit," Amalia said firmly. "Anna and Emilio are having a barbecue tonight, so all of the family can welcome our baby home. Be there at six."

Without allowing me another word, she turned and marched from my office. I could only smile and shake my head in admiration. It wasn't often that I had a case end so happily, so I had to enjoy it while I could. And what kind of Texas boy can turn down BBQ?

There was a box of tacks in my desk drawer, one of the myriad of office supplies I had purchased when starting the business that I'd never actually used. I took two, picked out a nice spot on the wall next to my framed license, and hung Penny's picture where I could always see it when I was sitting behind my desk.

My phone beeped to alert me that a text message had come in. *Pig Stand at 8 for breakfast and the real story*, it said. There was a little red heart at the end, and I couldn't keep a goofy smile from spreading across my face.

I hope you've enjoyed the first in the Jack Dahlish series. The story continues in MEMORY AND SORROW, when Jack's past comes back to haunt him.

Read on for a short story set two years before Lost Souls, as Jack and Nyk try to track down the creature killing people on a college campus.

Werewolf on Campus

I was in the middle of a dream that included a lot of turkey and pumpkin pie when an insistent noise pulled me into wakefulness. The buzzing paused, then started up again a second later. I pulled a pillow over my head in an attempt to drown it out.

When the buzzing finally stopped and I felt myself drifting back down into sleep, a loud chime jerked me awake again. I wanted to ignore that, as well, but there were only three people in the world set to ignore my phone's Do Not Disturb settings at night. None of them would be calling this late unless it was serious.

I groaned as I rolled over and patted around the bedside table until I found my phone sitting on the charging stand. Forcing my eyes open against the brightness of the screen, I stared at it for a few seconds until I could make out the words. Two missed calls and a voicemail, all from Ollie. The police sergeant usually worked the day shift, so whatever this was had to be important.

The voice mail played as I put the phone against my ear. "Jack, call me. Got something here that has to be one of yours. I hope to God this isn't the work of a human."

Lifting the phone away from my head, I squinted to make out the time. Just after two in the morning, a time when nothing good happened. I fumbled with the phone for a bit before managing to call Ollie back.

"Jack? You get my message?"

"Yeah, Ollie. What's going on?" That's what I was trying to say anyway. I'm sure my mouth got most of the syllables out.

"I'm at the UTSA campus, north of town. You need to get out here, Jack. This is a messy one." I could hear sirens in the background, and the voices of other police and crime scene techs as they passed by.

"Mmkay, give me half an hour."

I rubbed the sleep from my eyes as I padded into the bathroom. Ollie's tone told me it was urgent, so I settled for splashing water on my face before I pulled on a t-shirt and jeans. The weather was starting to turn colder, so I also grabbed a gray hoodie from where I'd dropped it a few days earlier.

Five minutes after waking, I was in my car and driving north. The roads were pretty deserted at that time of the night, so I was able to set my cruise control and speed along the highway as I wondered what could be so bad that it would freak Ollie out. After almost thirty years on the force, I didn't think there was much that could phase him.

As I pulled into the campus, it was easy to find the crime scene. Flashing lights lit up the night, and there were patrol officers blocking several streets. It took a few minutes of explanations before one of them allowed me to park just past his barricade.

Sergeant Oliver Williams was rumpled and wearing an expression of shock I'd never seen on his face before, when he arrived to escort me further into the blocked off area. "Thanks for coming, Jack."

His shell-shocked expression woke me better than the cold water had. "What's going on, Ollie? You look like a rookie at their first scene."

"I feel like one, too." He shook his head, wiping a sleeve across his mouth. "This one's bad, Jack. I don't know if I've ever seen a body this mangled outside of the worst traffic accidents."

He wouldn't say anything more as he led me past a dozen patrol cars, a couple of crime scene SUVs, and an ambulance with two paramedics sitting inside the open rear doors with vacant expressions.

A detective approached us, looking upset as he noticed my street clothing. When he recognized me, he looked even less thrilled. Most of SAPD knew that Ollie and I were friends, but the attitude toward private investigators was frosty, to say the least.

Ollie and the detective walked a few steps away to speak quietly. I'm not sure what my friend said, but the detective finally nodded grudgingly and shot me a disgusted look before he strode away.

"You're clear to take a look, Jack. Prepare yourself, because it is not pretty in there." He led me along a path to a small, wooded area bordered on three sides by sidewalks that led between campus buildings. "Couple of students were returning to their dorms around midnight. One of them had to take a piss after all the beer drinking, and he stepped off the path a few feet. When he found the body... well, I'm pretty sure those boys are going to need counseling for a while."

He glanced back at me, and I saw him swallow against the lump in his throat. The coppery smell of blood was on the air, growing stronger with each step as we entered the trees. After several more, Ollie stopped and turned away. His face was grim as he jerked his head for me to keep going.

I took another step hesitantly. Then another. Two people in blue coveralls were crouched down in front of me, but I could see dark splashes of blood all around. When I looked up, there were drops of the thick liquid on leaves far over my head.

One of the medical examiners glanced over her shoulder at me, as if wondering if I should really be there. Her shifting movement opened a gap for me to see what they were crouching over. Bile rose in the back of my throat and I raised a hand to cover my mouth.

The torso of the body was torn apart, almost shredded. Bits of organs were spread out for several feet in every direction, and my first thought was that a bomb went off inside of the poor guy. I forced myself to look closer, though, and saw ragged tears where something sharp tore through skin and ripped apart bone. Something that looked very much like large claws.

Ollie was standing outside of the wooded square as I stumbled out. I leaned over to put my hands on my knees, taking deep breaths of air that wasn't tainted with the smell of blood and organs. "You okay, Jack?"

"Me? That poor kid. What the hell happened in there?"

"I was hoping you'd be able to tell me. The detectives think it must have been a mountain lion that wandered in from the Hill Country."

The claw marks were large enough for the big cats. There had never been an attack by one in this area, though. At least not for the last forty or fifty years. Mountain lions tended to just eat small portions of their kills, too, not rip them apart as if for the fun of it.

"No way. If that were a wild animal attack, there would have been sightings in the area."

"Yeah." Ollie nodded, staring off into the distance. "So what does *that* tell you?" He tapped a finger against his chest, indicating the area where my talisman rested under my shirt. It was a silver chain running through a small hole in a large coin. The coin was pure silver, with gold inlay forming the profile of a man surrounded by words in a language no one had ever been able to translate. It was a Relic that gave me the ability to detect Filii Nox, supernatural creatures that lived among humanity.

"Aw, shit," I muttered, knowing I would have to go back into the clearing. Another thing the coin did was give me the ability to see essence trails left by Nox in the recent past. If I could detect one in the clearing, it would tell me if one of them was involved.

I took a steadying breath before pushing through the trees again. Stopping several feet away from where the medical examiners and crime scene techs still worked over and around the body, I reached a hand up to touch the talisman under my shirt. With an effort of will, I opened myself to the supernatural world.

Slowly, a trail of smoky essence formed through the clearing. It was too dark to see it beyond the limits of the portable lights focused on the body, but the essence was a murky shade of blue. Thicker around the corpse, with wisps of essence already drifting away as the wind and presence of so many people caused it to begin degrading. The smell that drifted into my nostrils alongside coppery blood was reminiscent of a dog, but wilder. Wolfish.

The nausea that always rose up inside of me while I opened my senses threatened to become overwhelming. When I was already queasy from the sight of the body, it was more of a risk than I wanted to take. I shut off my senses quickly, and almost ran away from the clearing.

"Well?" Ollie had his arms crossed, his lips tight under his black mustache as he stared toward one of the dorm buildings. Lights were on in many of the windows, with students staring out at the action of the police presence.

"Yeah, it's one of mine." I sighed. Whatever had killed this poor kid was my responsibility. The coin around my neck not only gave me the ability to see through the human masks the Nox wore, it made me the only person in the city that could protect humans when one of them broke the centuries-old Covenants by attacking innocents.

* * * * *

It was several hours before the crime scene people finished working the scene. My limited pass to view it didn't allow me to stay and wait, so Ollie and I retreated to an all-night diner down the road. He'd been off duty when he heard the call about the body being found, and something in the voice of the reporting officer had given him a gut feeling the attacker might not be human.

We drank coffee mostly in silence as we waited. Outside, a thunderstorm had rolled in. The rain and wind were probably causing all kinds of hell around the crime scene, and I was glad I hadn't chosen to stand outside the barricaded area to wait for everyone to leave.

He ducked out around five to call home and talk to his wife. As a cop's spouse, she was used to her husband being out all night now and then. But we both knew she'd worry if she didn't hear from him around the time she woke up to get ready for work.

"Sandra said you're coming over next weekend. We'll grill some fish, keep it healthy before the holidays." Thanksgiving was coming up soon, the meal I looked forward to most of the year. Not only for the great food, but for the childhood memories that were all I had left of family.

"Sounds good. How is she doing?"

"Good." He sipped coffee and then chuckled. "Starting to talk about doing this spin cycle nonsense. We don't even belong to a gym."

"Cardio is good for you," I said, eyeing his gut which had been expanding the last few years.

"Uh huh. You want to go run a few laps at the stadium, see which of us needs that cardio workout the most?"

I wisely kept my mouth shut, moving my eyes to watch the early news programs on televisions hanging nearby. "So much for keeping a lid on things."

Ollie twisted around to look at the tv I pointed to. One of the local stations had apparently been sent shaky cell phone footage from some students on campus. The angles weren't the best, but you could just make out some of the gore left behind from the attack.

"Great," he said as he turned back. "They'll have us guarding the scene all day now, to make sure the news people see how seriously we're treating this."

I winced, thinking that I might not get a chance to take a look at the scene in daylight, after all. "You, uh, couldn't get assigned to that, could you?"

He raised an eyebrow. "That's rookie work, Jack. Them and their poor training officers will get assigned to sit around and watch grass grow for a day."

"And I'm left trying to sneak in without being seen."

"I'm sure you won't be the only one," Ollie said. "If all those faces in the windows are anything to go by, those college kids are all going to be trying to sneak a peek."

A guess that proved correct when I headed back to the campus. I drove around for a while, getting a feel for where the cops had stationed themselves. Parking in an administration lot, I hurried across the campus on sidewalks that kept me away from police eyes. Not that I needed to worry.

Thirty or forty college kids were standing on the sidewalk surrounding the wooded square. With no classes that day, they had nowhere else to be. Yellow tape kept them back, along with three hard-eyed patrol officers who hurried over any time one of the students tried to get a closer look.

On the plus side, I didn't have to worry about the cops seeing me. I just wouldn't be able to get any closer to the crime scene. Even a rookie wouldn't let me past if I told them I was investigating the death.

Resigned to doing what I could, I touched my talisman. Doing so didn't help me open myself to the supernatural world any easier, but it had become an unconscious gesture. I didn't release it until the queasiness rolled in and I knew I was looking beyond the veil that hid the Nox from humanity.

Faint traces of the midnight blue essence were visible, but they were no more than small puffs of smoke here and there. The rain from the thunderstorm had washed most of it away, dissipating the essence as it would a scent trail for a dog. The heavy traffic of the students hadn't helped, either.

I tried to follow what was left of the essence trail, but it just led me in circles around the nearby buildings. I couldn't tell if this was the route the attacker had taken or just the areas they had travelled through leading up to the attack. I couldn't even guess at how old these traces were because they were degraded so much.

Grumbling in frustration, I returned to my car. I'd have to check in with Ollie later in the day, see if they'd managed to ID the victim. Perhaps checking their recent movements would give me a clue on why the attacker chose them. Unless this was some random opportunistic attack. In which case, I might never find out who did it unless they were stupid enough to have left a ton of physical evidence behind.

*   *   *   *   *

"Not a scrap of physical evidence," Ollie muttered. "The rain didn't help, but even before that the crime scene people couldn't find anything that would point to a specific suspect. Too much trash left on the ground by the college kids walking by every single day."

I leaned back in my office chair, looking out at the gray November day through the window. My small office suite was halfway up the building, giving me a view of a couple open-air parking lots, a smaller office building just past them, and the convention center beyond that.

"How about the victim? Did they manage to ID the poor guy yet?"

Loud honking made me pull the phone away from my ear for a second, and I heard Ollie talking loudly to someone as he covered his phone. "Sorry, Jack, there's been a bit of road rage out here, and I'm waiting for the tow trucks to get these cars off the road." His voice was muffled again as he told someone to focus on the road and drive.

"As to an identification, his name is Martin Corver. Freshman at UTSA, family lives a few miles west in the Hill Country. His parents came in and did the identification."

I could imagine all too well the pain they were feeling at the moment. I'd gone through something similar when my sister's body was found years earlier. That was when Ollie and I first met, the case that started me on a new path and revealed the existence of another world to the police officer.

"Do the detectives have any leads? People who didn't like Marty or something?"

"He was a quiet kid. His professors barely even realized he was in their classes, because he never spoke up or got himself noticed."

Ouch. That didn't speak well for them, but I knew how big those classrooms could be. Unlike high school, the students didn't show up every day, either. It would be easy to miss one face in that sea of rotating strangers.

"You're not giving me a lot to go on, Ollie. The scene was a total bust. Or it was from the closest I could get to it."

Ollie laughed. "Just a normal investigation, Jack. It's pretty rare to stumble upon that clue that solves the whole case. Have to do the grunt work to get there."

"Yeah, yeah." I turned back to my desk, where my laptop was running some searches online. I was looking for any recent attacks that might be related to this one. Murders with mutilated victims left behind, especially. I was running the search on the entire state, and there was a depressing number of results to sift through. "Guess I'll get back to grunting, then."

"I'll call you if I hear anything else, Jack."

After the call with Ollie, I was feeling pretty hopeless about finding a lead to follow on this murder. The only thing I had was the essence I'd detected early that morning near the body. My first thought was werewolf, but I knew the lycans received a lot more hate than they deserved. Hollywood made them out to be remorseless killers, but most were-creatures were quite docile. They had urges, like all of us, but contained them well.

In the time I had that thought, five more open cases popped up on the search results. Far too many people in this state died gruesome deaths, even if a lot of those were farm or traffic accidents.

Sitting there watching the results come in was depressing, so I pulled my hoodie on and left the building. I walked several blocks to go down a set of stairs to the Riverwalk. Even on a dreary November day, tourists were crowding the narrow paths along the river. Packing into the bars and restaurants that catered to them.

I reached my destination without having to think about it, going down the five worn stone steps that were so familiar after many years of frequent visits. The rusty steel door opened noise-lessly on well-oiled hinges, and I entered the confines of Lyon's Den. A small bar that was a haven for the Nox of San Antonio, and home to one of the people I called friend.

"Hello, Jack. I've still got a couple of organic burgers left, if you're here for lunch."

My stomach gurgled, demanding attention. "Sounds good, Richard. I'll have one."

He went into the small kitchen behind the bar to start on my order, but not before pouring me a pint of the local selection. Richard bought a keg or two of a different beer every couple of weeks, offering it as a rotating selection that I always tried out. This one had a hint of pumpkin and nutmeg, and I was ready for a second when he came back with a burger and thick-cut fries to put on the bar in front of me.

The Den was almost empty as I munched on my meal. A cou-ple of Nox sat at the far end of the bar from me, heads together in quiet conversation. One of them glanced over now and then, but I was used to that. Those who frequented the bar knew who I was, and most were wary of me the same way you felt cautious for no reason if a cop was nearby.

"You're working a new case."

I looked up at Richard in surprise. "What makes you say that?"

"You always get quiet when you have one. Too much internalizing." He smiled at me as he wiped the bar nearby. Richard had been an obsessive cleaner for as long as I'd known him.

"Well, now I'm going to be internalizing about how I internalize." I took another bite of the fantastic burger. "Did you hear about the body found out at the UTSA campus?"

"Ah," Richard said, throwing the white towel over a shoulder and leaning against the bar. "I thought the news reports were focusing on that one a little too much. Something strange about the death?"

"Just that the body was ripped apart. Blood and gore stretched out for several feet in almost every direction. It was... not pretty to look at."

"Any traces?" he asked, tapping his chest just as Ollie had at the crime scene very early that morning. Richard was the one who told me what the coin was when it came into my possession and helped me figure out how to use it.

I nodded as I chewed another bite. "Werewolf. I'm pretty certain on that."

"Hm." Richard looked over his shoulder at the other patrons, checking to make sure they didn't need his attention.

"What? Now I can see the internalizing going on in your head."

He snorted a laugh. "I was just thinking of something I heard last week. A family from out near Grey Forest were in, and I overheard them complaining about something attacking their animals. A few chickens went missing, then a goat turned up with its belly torn open."

"Oh." It wasn't uncommon for coyotes to attack animals in such a way, especially in a lightly populated suburb of the city. But that was awfully close to where the UTSA campus was located, enough that I didn't think it was coincidence. "Do you happen to know if there are any werewolf families living up there?"

"None that I'm aware of."

"Yeah, I don't know of any, either."

Lycans were often very insular, more so than most Nox. You might find a cluster of families living together that no one else was aware of, or that aren't seen away from their comfortable nooks more than once or twice a year.

In my eight years as one of the Nine, I'd encountered a were-creature only five times. One of them had been a werewolf, a woman I'd come across during an investigation into attacks on other Nox. She'd been pointed out as a suspect by one of the survivors, who said he'd butted heads with the werewolf several times. In the end, she'd been cleared by a simple interview. And she was probably the nicest of the people I'd had to talk to during that investigation.

"Guess it's time to start driving," I said, stuffing the last few fries into my mouth before I drained the remainder of my second pint. "I know a few other people out that way, so I'll check in with them."

*　*　*　*

I spent several hours that afternoon and most of the next day driving around the suburbs north of San Antonio. It was good to visit some Nox I hadn't spoken with in too long, but none of them had any information on werewolf families in the area.

As a last resort, I opened myself to the supernatural world as I drove slowly along back roads and country lanes. I was hoping that I'd spot some trace of a werewolf presence. Instead, I just ended up pulling to the side of the road to puke my guts out as my head pounded with a hammer beat.

After that experience, I decided to call it a day. There had been a full night without an attack, so maybe whatever creature had killed that poor college kid ran away when they realized what they'd done. Unlike in the movies, werewolves didn't need a full moon to shift their form, and they often didn't consciously realize what they'd done in their animal shape until after the fact.

The sun was setting behind the hills to the west as I pulled back onto the country road I was traveling. It was a beautiful sight, a good payment for all the time I'd been putting into the search. An image that stayed with me as I drove through San Antonio and pulled into the short driveway of my house.

I stumbled through the front door, dropping my hoodie just inside as I kicked my shoes off. Ollie hadn't called all day, so I pressed his name on my phone as I flopped onto the couch. While it rang, I turned on the tv and flipped through channels looking for anything interesting enough to take my mind off my worries.

"Sergeant Oliver Williams," he answered. He almost never answered that way when I called, which told me he was busy enough that he hadn't looked at the caller ID.

"Ollie, it's Jack. Anything new on the kid?"

"Hey Jack. Autopsy report came in this morning. Hard to tell when everything was so shredded and spread out, but a couple of organs seem to be missing from our victim."

I perked up. "Oh yeah? Which ones?"

"Heart and liver. But like I said, they could have just been scattered and weren't found yet."

That was interesting information. One of the things I knew for sure about werewolves was that they loved eating hearts. The blood-rich muscle was the first thing they dug out of a kill. The liver was the second favorite organ, based on accounts from past attacks on humans. That would seem to cement my idea of the type of Nox I was looking for.

"Find anything interesting on your end?" Ollie asked, breaking into my reverie.

"Not a damned thing. I'm pretty sure I know *what* killed the kid, but finding the specific Nox is proving to be a lot more difficult than I anticipated."

I heard the squeal of old chair wheels as he pushed back from whatever desk he was sitting at, then several seconds of echoing footsteps. "What are we dealing with here?" he finally asked, once he was in a place he couldn't be overheard.

"Werewolf," I said, finding a replay of an old Super Bowl game. It was one I remembered from my childhood, filled with player names I used to be able to recite from memory.

"What? Are you serious? Those are real?"

I laughed. "You should know by now, Ollie. If there's a myth or legend about it, then it's more than likely a species of Nox."

"Yeah, but... werewolves!"

"They get a bad rep, really. For no reason I can think of. It's like all those people who are afraid of sharks, even though the odds of being attacked by one are like one in four million. Something stupid high."

"But they're still sharks," Ollie said. "If you see one floating around, you get out of there as quickly as possible."

"Point."

"How many werewolves live in San Antonio, Jack?"

"Um, it's hard to say. Lycanthropes are very insular as a whole, so you often don't know they're around until you stumble across one."

"Ballpark it for me," Ollie said dryly.

"Maybe a dozen? Could be more, could be less."

He sighed, and I could picture him rubbing a hand across his face. It was late, so I knew he had to be exhausted and near the end of his shift. "And that's what we're dealing with here? How do I tell the detectives to look out for a big furry animal that might attack more students?"

"Well, the good news is that you probably won't have to. When werewolves do attack, they start small. Stray animals, goats, cows, that sort of thing. By the time they work up to humans, they're usually propelled by an impulsive desire to kill that's almost impossible to resist. The fact that there weren't any attacks last night makes me think they've pulled up stakes and gone somewhere else."

"That's not exactly good news, is it? Just means this thing could start killing in some place that doesn't have a person like you around to stop it."

Huh. I hadn't thought of that. "I'll keep my eyes open for any news reports of strange killings in the state."

"I'll do the same, but I'll also look at police blotters in New Mexico, Oklahoma, and Louisiana."

I yawned, pulling the phone away from my ear. "Sorry, it's been a long couple of days."

"I hear you, Jack. I'm still trying to catch up on my sleep from that night on the campus. Get some rest, and we'll talk in the morning."

There was no way I was going to argue with that. I had a quick dinner as I watched the third quarter of the old game, then dragged myself into my bedroom to fall onto the mattress. I was out before my mind had time to start obsessing over worries and concerns.

*   *   *   *   *

When the buzzing of my phone woke me this time, my eyes snapped open instantly. I grabbed the phone from the charger, seeing that it was just past five in the morning. Earlier than I liked to wake up, but I'd had enough sleep to feel mostly refreshed.

"Hello," I said into the phone.

"Jack." Ollie's voice was sleep-roughened, and he sounded strained. "It happened again. I just saw the report, a body found at the UTSA campus just after midnight."

I groaned as I rolled into a sitting position. "Crap. Same area? What did the victim look like?"

"I'm still reading the report," he said. I waited as he skimmed it on his laptop. Ollie was an early riser, often up at half past four.

216

Even on days off, he'd glance at the nightly reports for anything that might be of interest to me. "No photos attached to the report yet, but the crime scene drawings look very similar. Blood and viscera found up to eleven feet away from the body, the torso ripped open. Early indications that the heart couldn't be found."

The werewolf had struck again. I couldn't figure out why they would skip one night, when it was normally a consistent nightly pattern until they were caught or killed. I shuffled toward the bathroom. "I'll head out there in a bit, try to get a look at the crime scene. Send me anything new that comes in?"

"Will do, Jack. And be careful. The department is going to have a heavy presence after a second attack so soon."

I showered and dressed, walking through the front door fifteen minutes after the phone woke me up. It was the first day of the work week, so traffic was already starting to get heavy as I drove north across town. Another hour, and I'd have been slowed by several choke points where major roads intersected.

The campus was covered in patrol cars again, and I had to drive around for more than half an hour before I found a place I could park and walk to the latest crime scene. It was another secluded area, a restful place with a couple of benches surrounded by shoulder-height bushes to provide a slight privacy screen.

Four cops were standing in front of those benches, keeping back any curious passerby. I found a secluded place to observe them from a distance and saw a lot of college kids making three or four passes as they craned their heads to see past the officers.

My phone vibrated in my pocket, and I answered it quickly when I glanced at the caller ID. "Ollie, got something new?"

"Crime scene photos are coming in now. Remember how I told you the first one was messy?"

"Yeah."

"This one is ten times worse." His voice cracked and I heard a gulping swallow. "The bastard practically ripped her head off, Jack."

I grimaced, both at the image and the fact that our victim was a woman this time. "Another student?"

"No, this one was a professor. Young enough to be a student, though. It's her first year of teaching, and she's assisting several tenured professors in her department. Covering classes when they have other things on the schedule." He sighed heavily. "Twenty-five, Jack."

I knew what he was thinking about as he said it. Ollie's youngest child was the same age, though she lived out west. I could never remember where she'd ended up, but she'd gone to law school at a campus much like UTSA before she left home for good.

Giving him a few moments to collect himself, I did the thing I'd been dreading. I reached up to grasp my talisman as I opened my senses. The brightening morning quickly became darker as the midnight blue essence of the werewolf filled my vision. The Nox had been all over this area, though most of the essence was concentrated around the benches where the body was found.

There was something strange about it this morning. It felt wrong somehow. I stared at the essence trail for several seconds before seeing what my subconscious mind had picked up on. There were streaks of light gray throughout the essence today, which I hadn't seen the day before. Thin traces of the lighter color, but they were jagged and disconnected from each other by variously sized gaps.

"It's definitely a wolf again," I said into the phone. "Impossible to say if it's the same person, but I'd have to lean that way."

"How are we going to stop it, Jack? Before they kill another young person?"

I tried to determine the direction of the essence trail, somewhere I could trace it back to wherever the Nox had come from. The werewolf had moved in such an erratic fashion that the trail was entirely twisted in on itself.

"I'm going to have to call a friend," I said. "I know a guy who can help out. We'll find this thing before it strikes again, Ollie."

"Find them, Jack. And call me if you need another hand."

After ending the call, I stayed in my shaded spot and watched the cops as they shifted around. A pair of rookie cops appeared who seemed no older than the college kids trying to get a glimpse of the scene, taking the places of two others who looked relieved to be able to leave. They weren't taking any chances of someone wrecking the crime scene before they could be sure they had everything it might give up.

It was early, but I knew I needed to get a jump on this search while the trail was still fresh. I scrolled through my Contacts list and pressed the name of the person I was hoping would agree to help.

"Hello," the gruff voice answered. He'd been sleeping.

"Nyk, it's Jack. I've got a bad one, and I'm hoping you have a day or two to help me out."

"Just got in from delivering the latest bounty," he said matter-of-factly. Nyk Walsh was one of the best bounty hunters in the

States, probably the entire planet. Not only could he often track someone down who'd evaded a dozen large agencies, but he was also one of the few humans who knew about the supernatural Nox. Because of that, he was often hired to do jobs that regular bounty hunters couldn't be trusted with. He was in high demand, but often made time when I needed his help. We traded favors often. "Give me an hour, and I'll meet you."

"Thanks, Nyk." I told him how to find me on the campus, spotting the perfect place to wait for his arrival as I talked. Once the call ended, I jogged over to the small coffee shop that was just opening up. A line of half a dozen students had already formed, and I queued up with them.

I got the largest coffee available along with a blueberry muffin, and then was able to snag a small table outside where I could mostly see the crime scene. One of the cops walked over as soon as he saw the place opening, ordering regular coffees for all of the officers on guard duty. He ignored the questions the college students asked while he waited.

When Nyk arrived, he dropped into a chair next to me. It groaned in protest at having to hold him up. One of his ancestors had been an ogre, and the size and strength of that Nox had come to the fore big time after skipping a few generations. He stood a head taller than my six feet, with shoulders wide enough to need their own zip codes.

"So, what's going on?" Short and sweet, one of the things I liked about working with Nyk.

"Werewolf," I said quietly, making sure no one could overhear. "College kid torn apart late Friday night, and a young teacher in the wee hours this morning."

"Nothing Saturday night? That's odd."

"Yeah, I thought the same thing."

We were quiet as the cop walked past, carrying a small drink caddy with four tall cups on it. "I know a wolf down in Floresville. Are there any up here?" he asked.

"Not that I know of. I spent all of yesterday driving around hoping to find any traces of a family. No luck. Your guy in Floresville, do you think he might know others of his kind in the area?"

Nyk shrugged. "I can call and ask later. He's a night owl, though, sleeps until afternoon."

"Good plan B, in case we can't find any trail to follow here." I told him about the essence being twisted up so badly I couldn't trace where it had come from or where it might have gone.

"Let's take a look," he rumbled, pushing up from the chair. I tossed my trash as I followed him, wondering what he might see around the crime scene that I'd missed.

The cops guarding the area with the benches eyed the big man nervously, seemingly ignoring my presence entirely. I couldn't blame them. Nyk was the kind of person that drew your attention even when you weren't on the lookout for anyone trying to get past you.

He stopped a few paces away from them, not having to crane to see the reddish-brown stains that coated one of the benches and the ground around it. There were stains on the inner leaves of the surrounding bushes, as well. It was my first time getting to see more than tiny glimpses, while the officers were busy watching Nyk.

After a short time, he nodded at the two cops that had edged closer. Nyk turned to walk away from the scene, head down as he watched the ground in front of his feet. I followed again, trying to find whatever he was looking at without success. We walked past the large building, around the corner, and across a parking lot packed with vehicles.

Nyk stopped at the edge of the lot, his gaze rising to look through a screen of trees at the interstate not far away. "The wolf came through here," he said.

I looked around, trying to hide my confusion. "How do you know that?"

"The tracks," he said, waving at the ground. I bent closer to the ground, looking for anything that would stand out. Anything at all. Nyk laughed, crouching down to point out a faint impression in the ground beside the paving of the parking lot and then a small clump of dried mud a stride into the lot. "I saw more of this just beside the bench where the body was found."

"Huh. But couldn't it have been tracked in by someone else? A student, or a cop walking the crime scene overnight?"

"Could be, but the odds are good it's our wolf." Nyk placed his hand flat on the ground next to the faint impression. The footprint looked normal-sized, until I remembered just how large his hands were. "Big footprint, and yet they walked lightly. Students aren't usually that the self-aware, and cops tend to barge into everything since they're accustomed to being in charge."

Good reasoning, when I thought about it in that context. "So, we can keep tracking these footsteps, right? Go all the way back to wherever the werewolf came from?"

Nyk nodded, but his eyes weren't filled with certainty. "I can try. A lot of roads around here, though, and a smart person would travel across them in a way that would prevent someone like me keeping on their trail."

I waited in the parking lot as he pushed into the undergrowth of the green area that bordered the campus. I opened myself to the vision of the supernatural world, hoping for a stronger essence trail I could follow if Nyk lost the physical tracks. There was midnight blue smoke around the small, wooded area, but it was spread out and faint. It disappeared a step into the parking log on both sides of the trail. Passing traffic was one of the quickest ways to diffuse Nox essence.

Cars passed by now and then, and I got more than a few curious looks from the students and faculty behind the wheels. I almost expected one of the cops from the crime scene area to come over and ask why I was loitering there.

No one had appeared by the time I felt a hand on my shoulder. Jumping in shock, I turned to see Nyk standing beside me. I always forgot how preternaturally silent the big guy could be when he walked. He probably never would have left tracks to be followed.

"It's exactly what I was afraid of. I made it across the access road, tracked the trail under the overpass, but then I couldn't pick it up again beyond the westbound feeder lanes."

Whatever we were dealing with was aware enough to keep from being tracked then. Not a full-on wild werewolf, as I'd heard could happen every rare now and then. Mostly in regions with a lot more wilderness around them.

"We know it came from the north, at least," I said, looking that direction. It was the area I'd spent so much time driving around the day before.

"Possibly," Nyk said with a cautious tone. "Or they could have been traveling a roundabout path that originated south of campus."

I groaned, hating the wall I kept butting up against. "Well, call your guy in Floresville when you can. I'll keep trying to find werewolf families on my end." I glanced at the clock on my phone, noting the early hour. "I'm betting this Nox will attack again tonight. Since they seem to love the campus for some reason, want to meet me here at four? We'll do a circuit of the area before it's dark, and set up a place to watch from all night?"

Nyk nodded. "Good plan. I'll let you know if I find something before then."

He headed across the parking lot for a giant truck, the kind with two wheels on each side at back. It was jacked up a few feet off the ground, making it look normal-sized next to the giant bounty hunter as he pulled the door open and climbed in behind the wheel.

I jogged over to where my car was parked, having to pass the crime scene since I'd parked in another lot. The cops there eyed me uncertainly, and I raised a hand to wave at them. I appreciated the job they were doing, even if it was inconvenient for me personally.

The day passed quickly, without any success in tracking down werewolf families in town. I did come across a small group of werepanthers, who turned out to be standoffish but fairly nice once I introduced myself and told them what I was looking for.

They only knew of one other lycan group in San Antonio, and those weren't wolves, either.

After a late lunch that also subbed in for dinner, I headed back to the campus. Most classes were done for the day, and the parking lots were emptying out as I drove in. I grabbed a spot close to the crime scene from the previous night. I beelined for the coffee shop, managing to snag a large cup of go juice before they shut down for the day.

Nyk snuck up behind me again, making me spill some of the precious brown liquid when I jumped after he put a hand on my shoulder. He chuckled as I glared up at him. "Did you find out anything from your guy?" I asked.

He shook his head. "No luck there. His family doesn't socialize with others, so he doesn't know if or where other werewolf families might be."

About what I'd expected. Insular, remember? Lycan families were the definition of loners and hermits. Which made it all the harder to find the culprit in the rare cases where one of them started attacking humans or other Nox.

Nyk and I watched as the cops changed shifts again just before five. Only two young officers were left to guard the scene, so they must not have expected too many students to be out and about on a weeknight.

Once we saw that, we started our rounds of the campus. I kept the pace to a casual stroll, so that we wouldn't draw attention. Well, more attention than two guys in their thirties on a college campus would draw. Especially when one of them is big enough to be an NFL linebacker.

It took a little over an hour to complete a full circle as we wound between the buildings and around parking lots. There were too many places that would be ripe for an ambush by a creature hunting for prey. More than the two of us could hope to watch.

"We'll have to split up," I said. "You want the east, and I'll take west?"

Nyk nodded, pulling out his phone. "Call me if you see anything, Jack. You don't want to try and take on a werewolf alone."

I certainly didn't. My talisman might let me *see* the supernatural Nox for what they were, but aside from one instance on the first day I put it on, it didn't give me any special abilities to protect myself from them. I also disliked guns, which left me with few options for self-defense.

Nyk, on the other hand, was always ready for a fight. He had to be when he was chasing down bounties, even though he was the last guy I'd want to tangle with. He crouched down to pull a three-inch knife from a sheath in his boot, passing it to me before he turned and headed for his section of the campus.

I put the knife into the rear pocket of my jeans where I could reach it in an emergency, then stuffed my hands into the pockets of my hoodie and started patrolling my half of the vast campus grounds. It was getting colder as darkness set in, and I could already feel the caffeine boost from the coffee wearing off.

For the next three hours, I was constantly on the move. I used the flashlight on my phone to peer into any wooded areas or behind bushes and large plants, I stared across parking lots searching for the slightest movement, and I walked miles in a figure eight pattern. The moon rose above the campus buildings while I was making my rounds, half full and casting wan light across the grounds that competed with widely spaced streetlights.

*   *   *   *   *

I had fallen into a semi-dozing consciousness when a loud noise jerked my head around. It had almost sounded like a howl, but rougher and throatier. I pulled my phone out. "Did you hear that?"

"Yeah," Nyk said quietly. "Northwest of my location."

"Northeast for me," I said, already moving as quickly as I could without making too much noise. "Has to be our wolf."

Nyk didn't answer, but I could hear the wind blowing across his phone as he moved toward the sound. I was running across a vast parking lot, approaching a strip of trees, when I saw him coming from the opposite direction. He waved for me to stop, and I crouched to catch my breath until he was beside me.

"Did you see anything?"

"No," I said, shaking my head. "The howl had to come from here, though."

We both looked at the strip of trees. It was a bit of green space that separated the parking lot from the freeway access roads, perhaps twenty feet wide though it was easily a hundred feet long.

I led the way toward it, our heads on swivels as we searched for any movement and listened for any sound that might indicate something coming toward us. We entered at one end of the strip, moving through it with about six feet between us so that we could see the full width of the space.

By the time we reached the far side, I was more confused than ever. Nothing in there, and if the Nox had gone toward the campus we should have seen it crossing the parking lot. Nyk grunted when I asked for his opinion. "I saw tracks," he said, leading me back to where a few torn leaves were supposed to be the path the werewolf had taken through the trees.

"It would have crossed the parking lot, though, and we'd have seen it."

"Not if it moved fast enough," he said, looking toward the campus.

A second later a sharp crack filled the air. My ears perked up, and I saw Nyk's eyes tighten. "Gunshot," he said simply, before taking off.

I followed as quickly as I could, regretting my lack of cardio exercise as a stitch built up in my side halfway across the lot. We sped along the sidewalk on the far side, soon arriving at the open space where the previous night's kill had taken place.

"I swear," one of the cops was saying, his gun held out in front of him as he swiveled with wide eyes. "I saw it, right over there! It was a giant dog or something."

Nyk and I traded a glance, then looked in the direction the cop had indicated. The young woman standing beside him still had her gun holstered, and she was giving him a worried look. Her hand strayed up to the radio clipped to her shoulder and she spoke quietly into it.

"I'm not crazy!" the male cop said. "It was there."

We circled the area, keeping to the shadows so the spooked cop didn't fire off a shot in our direction. It took longer to get to the area where he'd seen what had to be the werewolf, but it was worth it to avoid getting shot.

Nyk crouched down, peering at the ground and running his hand over the grass near the sidewalk. "Something big came through here. This way."

I followed a few paces behind as he tracked the path of whatever had drawn the attention of the cops guarding the previous night's crime scene. I was glad neither of them had managed to get a good look at the werewolf. That was the last thing I needed to deal with.

Nyk raised a hand after several minutes, stopping me. Then he moved his hand forward, going through some rapid motions that I didn't understand at all. From knowledge gained while watching tv, I thought he was telling me the werewolf was close, but the rest of it could have meant anything from "it was here two days ago" to "it's eating you right now".

To be on the safe side, I reached back and pulled out the knife he'd given me earlier in the evening. Nyk pulled a heavy baton from inside his bulky windbreaker. There were wide rings of steel encircling one end, and I wondered how heavy the weapon would be before he even put his strength behind a blow.

He turned toward me, a whispered word escaping his lips. A white blur shot in from my peripheral vision, and in a second Nyk was gone. I twisted to find him on the ground, arms straining to hold back a snarling beast that had deadly claws sunk into one of his shoulders. The baton was nowhere to be seen.

This was only the second werewolf I'd ever seen, but the white fur was something I hadn't expected. They were usually a dark gray, like wolves you'd see in the wild. It took me too long to shake myself out of that fascinated observation.

Nyk was grimacing in pain as the wolf's claws sank deeper into the meat of his shoulder. I could see that arm weakening, even as the other tried to keep pushing the Nox away. I looked around wildly for a weapon, then remembered the small knife in my hand.

I darted forward, stabbing the knife into the side of the werewolf. It sank easily into flesh and muscle, and the beast let out a coughing yelp. A whirlwind seemed to envelop me, and a moment before I hit the ground I realized it had hit me hard enough to throw me through the air. The wind was knocked out of me, and my vision filled with stars.

The distraction had been enough for Nyk to free himself, though. He grunted as he shoved the beast aside and rolled out from under it, jumping to his feet. Blood was flowing from the wounds on his shoulder, but he ignored it as he set himself to meet the werewolf that pounced at him.

Nyk got two handfuls of fur, twisting his body to use the wolf's momentum against it. He tossed the beast aside, and it cracked into a thin tree trunk. The tree began to bend away from us as the werewolf pushed itself back up onto hind legs.

The wolf snarled as it began to circle the bounty hunter. It recognized him as the real threat between the two of us. As did I. The stars were fading as I pushed myself off the ground. My knife was still stuck in the wolf's side, and I didn't have a chance of even hurting it without a weapon. I looked around, hoping to find anything that I could use.

Moonlight glinted off metal, and I recognized the ringed baton Nyk had been carrying. It was lying near the tree that was now at a forty-five-degree angle. After a quick glance at the werewolf, I sprinted to it. In my peripheral vision, I saw the beast look toward me before leaping at Nyk.

The bounty hunter tried to catch and throw the wolf again, but it was ready this time. Claws raked across Nyk's chest, and he growled as he shifted to grab the werewolf's wrist and push it away from his body. The other claws came in lower, but Nyk was ready for that and batted the arm away. In the same movement, he slammed a fist the size of a small boulder into the bottom of the wolf's long jaw. The beast's jaws snapped shut with a loud click.

Nyk pulled his fist back for another blow, but the werewolf snapped forward to nip at his face. He had to pull back quickly, and the weight of the beast leaning into him pushed him off balance. He fell backwards onto the grass as I was scooping up the baton.

Or trying to. It weighed at least forty pounds, probably closer to fifty. I had to use both hands, and even then, it was a struggle as I start to drag it toward the fight.

The werewolf was pushing its advantage, jumping up to land with one hind leg on Nyk's chest as it continued trying to sink those sharp claws into his skin. The wolf's lips were pulled back in what looked to be a smile as it fought against the ogrish strength of the bounty hunter.

Nyk saw me coming from the corner of his eye, turning his head to look at me for a brief second before focusing on the wolf again. The hand closest to me flexed, opening and closing a couple of times. I knew what he was trying to say, and grunted as I strained to lift the heavy baton. With all of my strength, I tossed the weapon through the air.

Okay, so it was more like it skimmed the grass for a few inches before hitting with a dull thud and rolling. That was enough, though. Nyk gave a desperate push to create space between himself and the werewolf, then reached out to grab the baton. His hand wrapped around the leather-wrapped handle.

The baton whistled through the air, thudding against the werewolf's shoulder. It yelped in surprise and pain, tossed to the side by the weight of the blow. Nyk sucked in a deep breath before he rolled to push himself up, the only sign of the toll the attacks were taking on him.

The werewolf was righting itself at the same time, rear legs bunching as it prepared to leap at Nyk again. I shouted a warning, but he kept his eyes on the ground as he got his feet set. The white wolf surged forward, streaking across the gap between them.

Nyk raised the baton with lightning speed, the heavily weighted end slamming into the side of the werewolf's head. The beast took a few lurching steps away from the bounty hunter, landing with a sickening thud between Nyk and I.

I held my breath as I watched, wondering if the wolf was still alive. That blow had been solid, and I didn't imagine a human could have survived it. Nyk was watching for the same thing, standing with the baton hanging loosely at his side.

A whuffing sound came from the wolf, then it twitched. An arm shifted, then was still. I released my pent-up breath, looking uncertainly to Nyk. He shrugged, taking one step forward. He paused, waiting for a reaction, then took another.

Without warning, the werewolf rolled. It lunged forward, jaws open as it strained to get a hold of Nyk. He raised the baton in an instinctual reaction, dropping it to slam against the top of the wolf's head. The jaws clicked closed inches away from Nyk's leg as it dropped to the ground again.

This time we waited longer, several minutes passing as we looked for any sign of life from the beast. Nyk was stepping forward to check on it when a car screeched to a stop nearby. I turned to look in that direction, seeing a man perhaps ten years older than me come running.

"Dad!" he yelled. "What did you do to him? Dad!"

He dropped to his knees beside the white werewolf, lifting the massive head to his lap. His shoulders were shaking as he sobbed, rocking back and forth.

Nyk and I traded a glance over his head, and I crouched down. "You're a werewolf, too? Was this your father?"

The man nodded, not looking up. I reached out to put a comforting hand on his shoulder, but he flinched away. "Dad," he moaned, pulling the limp werewolf tighter against his body.

I coughed to clear the lump in my throat. "Did you hear about the people killed on campus the last several nights, sir?"

He nodded again. When he spoke, his voice was so faint I had to lean in to catch his words. "We tried to keep him locked up. I thought we could, but then he got out last night. And tonight. He doesn't know what he's doing." The man looked up at me, his sad eyes meeting mine. "Dad keeps getting lost in his memories. I swear to you, he wouldn't kill if he were still in his right mind."

Nyk grunted, backing away from us. He and I could both tell the werewolf wouldn't be getting back up. Whatever old memories had driven him to give in to his animal urges and kill would no longer afflict him.

"We didn't have a choice," I said. I think I was talking more to myself than the mourning son, but he nodded. "He would have killed again, and we didn't have a choice."

"I know."

I backed off to give the man time to grieve. It wasn't as much as I would have liked, though, as flashes of light drew my attention. Someone must have heard the noise of the fight and was coming to investigate. Nyk gave me a gentle shove toward the werewolves, taking off to try and delay whoever it was.

"We need to get him out of here," I whispered, bending down next to the man. "If anyone finds him here, like this..."

"It would be bad," the man agreed, sniffing and running a hand across his eyes to wipe away tears. "Help me."

Together, we lifted the werewolf and carried him towards a small car parked half in the grass nearby. The beast felt so frail in death, and I reflected that the fur must be white from age. We managed to get the wolf onto the back seat of the car, and I shut the door as the man hurried around to the driver's side.

He stopped to look at me over the roof of the car. "I understand why you did it, Dahlish. But I'll never be able to forgive you for killing my father."

So, he knew who I was. "I get it," I said. "But there were two people dead, killed in a horrible fashion. I didn't have much choice. It was your father, or an untold number of others before the cops caught up to him. We both know how disastrous that would be."

His jaw clenched, but he nodded. Many of the Nox were more afraid of humanity stumbling across their true nature than I was. They remembered what it was like before the Covenants created peace, a respite from centuries of constant fighting and prejudice. Many feared being hunted again, just because they looked different from the mass of humanity around them.

The car backed up quickly, then drove away across the parking lot as fast as it could go. The taillights were just disappearing behind a building as running footsteps came to a stop beside me. I looked over to see the young female cop who had been guarding the crime scene earlier.

"What's going on over here?" she asked, shining a flashlight in my face.

"Nothing," I said, raising a hand to shield my eyes. "My friend and I were just having a little disagreement. Not a big deal." I looked over to where Nyk was speaking with the other cop. For a moment, I wondered who was supposed to be watching the crime scene.

She stared up at me with a frown, clearly wanting to make a big deal out of it. The radio on her shoulder squawked, though, and that reminded her what she was supposed to be doing. The cop did a full circle with her flashlight, looking for anything that might give her cause to question me further.

"It's late," she said before walking away. "You and your friend need to get inside. Now."

"Yes, officer."

As she passed, she pulled the male patrolman away from Nyk. The young idiot had his face up as close as he could get to the man that towered a head and a half over him, his mouth working as he spat words. Nyk gave me a glance as the cops walked away, rolling his eyes.

"How is the son doing?" he asked as I walked over.

"As well as he can." I sighed, rubbing my back where I'd landed after the werewolf knocked me away. "I hate that we had to kill the old guy."

"He didn't give us much choice," Nyk said, putting a heavy hand on my shoulder.

"I know, but there has to be a better way. You know?"

That was the one thing I always came to at the end of cases like this. Why couldn't there be a way to try and help the Nox who broke the Covenants? Those who attacked or killed others and had to be stopped in the only way available to me? Sure, sometimes I could turn them over to human law enforcement, but only when I was sure they wouldn't expose the truth of what they were, and they couldn't hurt those trapped behind bars with them.

"The important thing is that the people on this campus are safe tonight," Nyk said, pulling me along as he started walking toward the lot where we'd parked. His jacket was ripped where the werewolf's claws had swiped at him, but the blood that had poured from the wounds was hard to see against the dark material. Without that, we'd probably be in the back of a police car answering questions.

"Yeah, the kids can sleep safe." I looked at the buildings around us. The dorms had a few lit windows, but most were dark so late on a weeknight. Studying was done, and they were dreaming of better lives once they got their degrees.

My phone rang, and I looked down to see Ollie's name on the display. I smiled, glad I'd have a little good news to lighten his worries.

"Hey, Ollie. The problem is taken care of."

About the Author

After more than 20 years of working IT support for a nationwide bank, I decided it was finally time to start putting my imagination to the page. Creating stories and new worlds has been second nature for me since I was a kid, and I've wanted to be a writer since high school.

Please leave a review if you've enjoyed this book. Or even if you haven't. Reviews not only help me to improve my writing, but they let other readers know if they might want to read the book.

If you'd like to keep up to date on my projects, visit my website at www.timrangnow.com. You can sign up for my monthly newsletter there, and you'll get access to exclusive short stories and early peeks at upcoming books.

Dahlish Series

Lost Souls
Memory and Sorrow
Dark Deception
Fateful Knights

Other Books by Tim Rangnow

Guild Series

Vagabond
Indomitable
Waterloo
Resolute

Rim Jumper

Prime Example
Viridian Skies

Printed in Great Britain
by Amazon

11078586R00140